I0542460

A TEA PARTY
&
OTHER STRANGE STORIES

AARON M. WILSON

AN EVERYTHING FEEDS PROCESS BOOK

Copyright

ISBN: 978-1-300-23836-2

Published by Everything Feeds Process Press, Minneapolis, MN

Copyright © 2012 by Aaron M. Wilson.

The stories in *A Tea Party & Other Strange Stories* by Aaron M. Wilson are licensed under the Creative Commons Attribution-NonCommercial-NoDerivs 2.0 Unported License. To view a copy of this license, visit http://creativecommons.org/licenses/by-nc-nd/2.0/ or send a letter to Creative Commons, 171 Second Street, Suite 300, San Francisco, California, 94105, USA.

- "The Lily Pad." *eFiction Magazine: The Premier Internet Fiction Magazine*. Vol. 15. Ed. Doug Lance. Web. 1 June 2011

- "The Return of Melanoplus Spretus." *eFiction Magazine: The Premier Internet Fiction Magazine*. Vol. 12. Ed. Doug Lance. Web. 1 March 2011

- "The Birthday Party." *Evolve*. Ed. M. Chase Whittemore. Web. 18 October 2010.

- "Alhazred's Walls." *eFiction Magazine: The Premier Internet Fiction Magazine*. Vol. 7. Ed. Doug Lance. Web. 1 October 2010

- "The Methuselah Project." *The Hive Mind*. Ed. Alexandra Wolfe. Web. 18 June 2010.

- "Keeping Watch." *eFiction Magazine: The Premier Internet Fiction Magazine*. Vol. 3. Ed. Doug Lance. Web. 2 June 2010.

- "Running of the Cows." *eFiction Magazine: The Premier Internet Fiction Magazine*. Vol. 3. Ed. Doug Lance. Web. 2 June 2010.

- "A Tea Party." *eFiction Magazine: The Premier Internet Fiction Magazine*. Vol. 3. Ed. Doug Lance. Web. 2 June 2010.

Cover Art: Copyright © 2012 by Kristen Nelson.

Disclaimer:

These stories are works of fiction. Names, characters, places, and incidents are the product of the author's imagination or are used fictitiously, and any resemblance to actual persons living or dead, business establishments, events, or locals is entirely coincidental.

Acknowledgements

Many of the these stories would not have been possible if not for the time and space given me by Hamline University in St. Paul, MN, during the completion of my *Master of Fine Arts in Writing*. However, please do not blame either the university or my thesis advisor for the strangeness of the content or the quality of story, which are completely my fault.

eFiction Magazine and its editor Doug Lance also deserve acknowledgement. When I felt like no one would ever publish or read my work, Doug read them and eFiction Magazine gave many of them their first home.

The stories in this collection that are new to the world would not be so without the help of a dedicated writers group. Thank you: Darci Schummer, Todd Wordrope, Matt Johnson, Judy Johnson, and my wife, Jessica Fox-Wilson.

Lastly, I would like to thank my daughter, Nora, for allowing Daddy the time to be strange in-between storybooks, meals, naps, and bedtimes.

For

Nora Rose Wilson

Table of Contents

Keeping Watch

One

This is the 12th year after the completion and settlement of Satellite State—258. Those with money and influence have long since moved into one of the 258 Satellite States that fill the sky. They have escaped into perfectly controlled communities, where the weather is always nice and the air and water recycled, scrubbed, cleaned, purified, and pumped back into the enclosed system they now call home. For them, hunger, disease, and war are now only concepts of a brutal Earth-bound past, studied by SS children in history books and old movies.

Those that do not posses either influence or wealth still reside on Earth. The lucky have found work on one of the many corporate farms that produce much of the resources needed to sustain the Satellites.

There they are forced to work long hours with less than adequate tools, for two meals a day and a bunk, in what amounts to nothing more than one of the many rows of poorly kept machine sheds. Their names have been taken and replaced with a number designation that has been encoded and tattooed as an easily readable barcode on the underside of their left forearm.

And then there are those who still live in what are left of the Earth's cities. The cities continue to shrink in order to make way for more farmland. Those who live in a city are mostly jobless. Those that do work have been lucky enough to have signed on to one of the thousands of F.M.U.s (Flexible Maintenance Units) that commute in shifts to one of the 258 Satellite States. There, they sweep, recycle, bus tables, and wash everything from windows, dishes, and clothes to walkways and buildings. They too have given up their names for encrypted barcode tattoos that entitle them to food rations and just enough credits to live in run down apartments on Earth.

Everyone that is not already living in one of the 258 satellites is attempting to find a way off the surface of the Earth. There are only two possible ways to take up residency in one of the Satellite States, the I-140 Immigrant Petition for Alien Workers and the I-130 Immigrant Petition for Alien Relatives. However, there are those that have found a third alternative to the two legal channels of immigration and then there are those who help them through subversive acts. It is my job to police, watch, if you will, the citizens of one of the 258 satellites. What follows is the sad story of someone who should have known better.

Two

Randal Haus smiled. He had just inspected, and ultimately denied, another poorly executed I-140. His tenth denial today. Haus made smiling a part of his job. After each application, he'd stand, stretch, and smile, before opening and inspecting the next I-140. He was very proud of his routine. He had come up with it on his own. It was his, and he'd been asked to teach it to his peers. His immediate supervisor had noticed a few months back that he'd increased his productivity by more than twelve percent. However, when Haus had explained his success to his supervisor, she had merely chuckled.

A few weeks had passed before he had been awarded Employee of the Month for excellence in productivity. Soon after, he had been asked to prove his technique against another group of high performers. While the others tore through application after application, Haus took a few seconds in between and performed his routine. While the others had completed more I-140s than Haus, their applications were found to have errors and oversights. One of his competitors, George Strap, had even granted a visa to an unsponsored, unskilled Earth Number. Very embarrassing for Strap, but for Haus, it had ensured victory. Haus may have only completed forty to their fifty-five each, but his I-140s were clean. The average Satellite State Immigration Specialist could only complete thirty-two I-140s in an eight-hour day. Now, everyone who inspected and processed the I-140 Immigrant Petition for Alien Workers, had to practice *The Haus Technique*.

Three

Errors. So many errors. Haus took joy from his work like no other. He lived to reject applications. However, nothing brought him more satisfaction than being able to process a perfect I-140. The management felt that certain errors were acceptable, misplaced commas, spelling, first name in the last name field and last name in the first, etc. He had been told that those types of errors could be overlooked.

The kinds of errors that caused an application to be rejected were bigger, no application fee attached, no personal identification code, bad address, unexplained gaps in employment. One error that was common and that would land anyone in the rejected file was incorrectly listing your family history. Many of the applicants had protesters or runners, illegals caught loose in a Satellite State, in their immediate or extended family. It was a mistake to not list them. Just because someone had a bad egg or two would not immediately result in a rejected application. Most would be rejected eventually, but there were applicants whose circumstances warranted acceptance.

Haus had one of those on his desk. The application was perfect in every way. The penmanship was even superb. It was from a self educated Earth station worker named Carlos Hernandez. He had taken the time to list each and every relative. Among them was a sister who had escaped from her F.M.U. I like to imagine that Haus had an active dream life. In reality, I think that Haus wouldn't know a wet dream if it tickled him. However, if he did dream about his work, he dreamt about the sister in this application.

Two women huddle together in a dark forgotten corner of SS—62. They've been taking turns sleeping and keeping lookout. They don't speak out loud, but with their hands and their eyes. They've been moving through service and waste tunnels. Each knows that the other is hungry, tired, and scared. They don't need to say it, but it's been several days, and if they don't find help and food soon, they might miscarry.

They carry the hopes and dreams of so many in their wombs. They know that they cannot fail, but don't know what their next move should be. They were told that they would find help if they looked for it. Except that when their opportunity presented itself, they had only seen a middle-aged man who didn't look helpful. In fact, they thought they had heard him calling the cops as they ran down a Main-way and then a Side-way through rows of homes.

In the dark quiet, one of the two women rolls up her left sleeve past her elbow. She looks at her barcode number—4.5.7.9.1.4.3.3.4.2.9.0.0.0.0.E115—her name, her purpose, her life. When someone had given her direction, they'd yell, "four-of-E-one-one-five." She traced its lines with her finger and tried to remember what her mother had called her. It had been so many years since she'd needed a real name. She looked at her companion and thought that they should use real names with each other. But who was her companion? She didn't know anything about her. They had been paired because they were in their first trimesters and they weren't showing yet. It had taken a lot of money to bribe all the right people, including their F.M.U. handler. The riot the others had started had been all for show—to keep the handler from losing his job, and keep the opportunity for other runners alive. The F.M.U.s expected runners. As long as it was under a certain percentage, no one asked questions.

As she rolled her sleeve down she thought about her unborn child and the life it would have. She secretly hoped for a boy. With a boy there would be less chance that her child would be sold into prostitution by the delivering doctor or midwife. The worst that a boy would have to endure would be hard labor in one of the solar collection teams. An SS birth guaranteed SS citizenship, but once her child turned eighteen he'd have to find work. And if his test scores didn't qualify him for something good, he'd be placed. That was an orphan's lot, and *if an illegal's orphan needed to be placed, the government would make sure that they were not in a position to easily help other illegals.*

Yes, she wanted a boy. She put her hand under her shirt and moved it soothingly over her abdomen murmuring, "Fernandito, Fernandito, Fernandito."

The other woman is sleeping soundly; Haus enters her dream of raising her child in the comfort of outer space. She saw herself in a nice blue dress holding her baby in her arms feeding it an afternoon bottle. Life seemed perfect. Her husband owned a small but successful restaurant in the entertainment zone, a real nice family kind of place. She knew deep within her soul that her baby would grow up and take over the restaurant and have lots of grandchildren for her to keep watch over. Still soundly asleep, she rolled over, closer to her companion, putting her arm around her as if she were her husband and they were in love.

I like to think that after a dream like that Haus would wake and not be able to sleep. His insomnia led to his need to fill night cycle hours, which led to the creation of "The Haus Blog," a throwback to another age, but simple enough for anyone to learn quickly. He started out with the typical self-indulgent nauseating biographic information about his everyday life: food he ate, places he visited, stuff that he liked to read.

Then one night the content changed.

Four

Randal Haus sat in his supervisor's office. He looked confused. He had work he needed to do. He couldn't for the life of him figure out why she needed to see him, and why she had security escort him into her office. He was getting nervous.

"Randal," she had begun, "Randal. Randal." She had paused seemingly to let Haus stew a bit. A pause she lengthened by re-applying her rusty-red lipstick and then making uncivilized popping sounds with her lips.

Haus waited. He knew his place. He knew that if she had wanted him to say something that she would have asked a question. To bide the time, he looked inward and held his hands in his lap. He thought about all those people whose I-140s would not be processed or rejected today because he was sitting in here, waiting, watching his supervisor apply lipstick. He hated the way some people could just ignore that other people were watching them. Worse yet, they wanted other people to watch, or in his case, forced them to watch. It made him mad.

Haus liked being mad. There were many things in this world that made him mad. He thought about his most recent blog post. Posting helped. It was an outlet. He had read somewhere that typing out your frustrations was a way to be angry without being angry.

His latest post had been about the time he had been walking down the street where a F.M.U. had been cleaning the public green space. It had only been a few days ago. He had stopped to watch them. They were so short and so brown. They had spoken a dirty, crazy sounding language. The men had short hair or shaved heads, while the women had long dark brown or black hair, which they kept in braids or tied back with scarves. The F.M.U. Handler had been standing on one of the many red picnic tables. A couple of the older F.M.U. men had started making a scene. They had stopped collecting leaves and were swinging their rakes over their heads and hitting each other.

Haus had looked on as the F.M.U. Handler had gotten down off the picnic table and tried to break up the fight. Haus then noticed that two of the F.M.U. women had dropped their rakes and were running toward him. Before Haus had a chance to call out, the two women had disappeared down an alley. Haus then did what any noble SS citizen had to do. He had called the police. They had taken his statement and ensured him that they would be caught and deported back to Earth where they would be imprisoned without parole for a year and then assigned to a farm.

Knowing that the F.M.U. runners would be punished did not abate Haus' anger in the slightest. He knew that many runners were never found and that the majority of the runner-women would be with child, and children born in a Satellite State were given automatic citizenship. Their mothers were still deported, but a child born in space must live its entire life in space. Haus didn't know the specifics, but he knew it had something to do with a post-natal syndrome caused by birth outside Earth's gravity. And these syndrome-children didn't need to file an I-140, and eventually, when they turned eighteen, they could file an I-130 request to bring their immediate family to come and live with them.

If Haus thought too much on the subject, he'd eventually go crazy; and Haus knew that crazy couldn't process an I-140. So he turned his thoughts back to his supervisor.

"What are you snarling about?" His supervisor was standing now. "You're being let go, Randal." She moved out from around the desk, her heels clicking on the tile floor. "Do you know why? Randal did you see the man in the dark suit who left as you came in? He was some kind of government agent. He had a badge that I'd never seen before. I even made some calls, Randal. I made calls for you."

Haus sat there stunned. Fired. He was being fired. The Haus was being fired.

"Randal are you listening to me?"

"Fired?"

She sat down in her overstuffed office chair behind her desk. She looked Haus in the eye. "Randal." She straightened up. "Randal, you're officially being let go because your numbers have dropped and you are unable to provide the productivity necessary to remain in your position." Haus' supervisor looked right at him. "Officially, you were warned. Officially, we gave you ample opportunity for improvement." She looked toward the door. "Unofficially, you were the best and most efficient. Unofficially, you fucked up big time." She shook her head. "Your blog, Randal, your blog."

Haus thought about those two F.M.U. women. He knew that somehow this was their fault. Losing his job was their fault. He hadn't been himself since he'd seen those two women. Then he asked, "My blog?"

His supervisor interrupted, "Randal, don't you get it? Are you that special? Wait! Don't answer that." She paused, shaking her head. "I need you to clean out your desk immediately." She walked back around her desk and opened her office door. "Oh, and just in case you haven't caught on, don't ask for recommendations. You got that, Randal?"

It was true. Haus didn't understand. All Haus ever wanted in life was to process properly completed I-140s.

Five

That night Haus sat in front of his computer after eating a nice dinner. He was mad. He wanted to do something. He wanted to take action. He had a helpless feeling. It was a feeling that there were people in the world that could one day show up and ruin everything. It was a feeling that Haus didn't like. It was an accurate feeling.

Haus picked up where he had left off on his blog. I'm convinced that he didn't know that what he was writing was dangerous and subversive. I still don't think that he had a creative side. Some people were born to build spreadsheets and crunch numbers and Haus was one of them. He was born to process paperwork. He was not, by all accounts, born to write creatively or hypothetically, which only left his experience, what he knew. And what he knew was dangerous.

What Haus did know was that he liked his new outlet. He had readers. He had a lot of readers who liked to comment and ask him questions. Haus liked the questions the most. He would spend hours crafting answers to those questions. These answers put him to the top of my list, a list that no one wanted to be on, a list that I did not want him on.

Six

Randal Haus sat in the park. He must have been thinking about his lost job, his life, and those two F.M.U.s. No matter how hard he tried, he couldn't stop thinking about them. He knew all the statistics about F.M.U. runners, their chances of survival. One percent. It gave him some satisfaction knowing that they would probably be dead. One percent would find help and bring their children to term. One percent still seemed too high.

It'd been three months since he'd seen them, one since he'd lost his job and had to settle for a low-level gig. His new job actually paid about the same, but it seemed so less important, monitoring the axis lubricant levels of SS 62's 3rd environment-ring, panel number 5. If the levels ran too hot (which they never did) or too low (which they never did), he'd need to issue the request for maintenance. His new supervisor explained that if either situation ever occurred, the 3rd ring would lose artificial gravity as it ground to a halt. The whole process was run by a computer; his position was just a precaution. He would laugh, but it paid the bills, and paying bills was no laughing matter to Haus.

So, to keep his mind busy he continued to work on his blog. He worked on his blog to keep himself awake as he watched lubricant levels scroll by on his monitor. His supervisor had actually encouraged him, claming that his employees who multitasked showed better reaction times.

While Haus sat in the park watching the birds, he looked at his latest entry on his data pad. His blog was getting even more attention. If he couldn't process applications, he would help fill them out. Immigration aid was expensive and did not always guarantee citizenship. If an applicant followed his free advice, they were sure to be put through.

I-140, Section 3.1: Background Checks

This section is where an applicant can either make or break his or her I-140.

This section is totally out of human hands.

The computer takes over once the specialist has entered all the applicants listed reference numbers. As long as the applicant's numbers and the numbers of relatives logically fit into the not so complicated identification evolution program, the applicant clears.

Common Mistakes

applicant misfiles a number

applicant files a non-blood relative

applicant files a blood relative who is a felon

applicant leaves out the three digit SS or E code

applicant used a pencil and the number has become unreadable

Haus had never expected to be approached by a publisher. He looked at the email again on his data pad to confirm that this was the correct park and the correct time. While he waited, he dreamed of breaking into the top 50 blogs of all time by the end of the year. Perhaps, if he distilled the site down to just information on the I-140 and I-130, deleting out his more journal-like entries about how his day had been and where he had eaten lunch, he could move his rating a few notches by the end of the next season-cycle.

Haus looked at the time. The publisher was now very late. Haus was beginning to get agitated. He had to quiet his mind. He had been taken to daydreaming as of late as a way to calm himself. He missed the meditation that processing applications had brought him. But before he could relax he heard me say, "Randal Haus," as I extended my hand.

He took my hand and shook it. "Yes."

"May I sit next to you?"

"Yes, please." He sat back down with the biggest, widest, cow-eyed grin. "It was getting late. I didn't think that you were going to make it. I have some great ideas for a book." He opened a file on his data pad. "Let's see. Oh, yes. I think that I will open with a..."

He felt me stick the needle in his arm. His eyes were crystal-blue. I whispered gently, "Randal Haus, you have been found guilty of High Treason, for the act of distributing highly classified information." He slumped into my lap, eyes still opened. I help him sit up straight, tilted his chin down, and folded his hands in his lap.

Aaron M. Wilson

The Lily Pad

When wishing for things was still in fashion, there lived a self-professed fairy-princess, who was neither fairy nor royal born. Moreover, there was nothing remotely magical about her person. She was, simply put, just another tall sandy-blonde from Los Angeles, who applied a glittery rainbow of color to her otherwise befreckled and chalky palate. Thus, the only apt comparison between her and fairy royalty was that she left a fine trail of glittery dust in her wake. As she left the limo with her girlfriend-entourage, she wasted a wish to cut the club's queue, a wish that, if left unmade, would have prevented her tragic fate.

To help her misspent wish along, her girlfriend-entourage formed up behind her. With two flowery dressed glitter-bombs flanking her on both sides, she signaled their approach. Together, they catwalk stomped in V-formation, hips swaying and heals clicking, up to the overly large doorman. As expected, her wish was fulfilled. Moreover, as she and her girlfriend-entourage cut the queue into the newest haute dance club in town, she was singled out by doorman. He gave her a muddy-green card that read, *Lily Pad: Dance Floor*, in neon-yellow and told her to see the bartender. Without thinking twice about it, because not only did such things happen to her often, she expected them, she slipped the card into her rhinestone clutch. She then puckered her pouty-pink lips and blew the doorman a kiss as she flipped her hair over her bare shoulders in a storm of cinnamon, ginger, and glitter. Entranced, the doorman lingered a second too long in the shower of gingerbread-scented sparkles that he allowed the entrance of the one creature he was told, specifically, to guard against.

Sliding under the rope and behind the doorman, a the child-sized creature known to the club's owner as Batrachos entered unnoticed. Batrachos had been a man once. Handsome, strong, a real lady's man, but he had had the misfortune of catching the owner of Lily Pad's eye. The owner was a *real* witch, and she was not used to having her advances ignored. To repay him for the slight, she had turned him into a hideous bullfrog and banished him from her establishment.

Inside, the scene was not unlike other ultra-exclusive dance clubs. The music was overly loud sugary-pop with a thumping undercurrent of bass that sent ripples across a water-filled center stage shaped like a Lilly pad. Swimming all around the stage were exotic looking frogs. A multi-spectrum strobe light lit the smaller elevated center stage, which was occupied, solely by the self-professed fairy-princess.

She held her stilettos, one in each hand, by the heel, as she danced and splashed in the small center stage pond. The water was warm and a little more than a foot deep so that as she danced, water splashed over the sides and the tips of her flower shaped skirt darkened and clung to her legs. The spilled water ran down the sides of the elevated dance floor into a ring cut into the floor and was recycled back up into the pool where she was oblivious to the child-sized bullfrog dancing at her feet.

The music transitioned from one of her favorite songs to another. Finding the beat, she moved her body with renewed fervor. Hands over her head, she jumped, let out a particularly girlish squeal of delight, and snaked her body in such a way that her tear-shaped rhinestone clutch, precariously sharing space in her right hand with a stiletto, fell into the water. The clutch quickly found its way to one of the water recycling pumps and disappeared.

Now, the self-professed fairy-princess could have done without the majority of the clutch's contents, such as her Kat Von D *Hustler* lip-gloss and *Techno* mascara, her extra dose of *E*, her Astroglide lubricant, and her I.D, but her most prized possession was also safely contained therein: her Apple iPhone. Desperately, she got down on her hands and knees in the small pool and groped for it. Seeing that the clutch, along with her phone, was beyond her reach, tears left dark mascara streaks on her otherwise luminous cheeks.

As she was crying, the unnoticed creature lifted a sticky webbed hand and brushed a tear from her cheek. Then he croaked, "What ails the prettiest of the pretties? Thy tears would move the most heinous of flies to pity."

Startled by the sudden appearance of the child-sized frog, she pulled back from its webbed hand. It was a hideous deformed thing, definitely not man-shaped but not entirely frogish either. It had the wide set bulbous eyes, smooth greenish and brown skin, webbed and padded feet of a frog, but its lips and mouth didn't seem quite right. Then, while they eyed each other, its long sticky tongue shot out to the left before quickly retracting. Still waiting for an answer, the frog seemed to chew and swallow what ever its tongue had caught. After the initial shock of not only meeting a talking frog but also being touched by one, she remembered that she was used to men, all men, offering to perform all manner of services for her. She also remembered that she knew how to use men. Seeing a lucky circumstance, she took advantage. She lowered her elongated and rainbow-shaded lashes over her eyes, and she tilted her chin over her shoulder.

"I've lost my clutch. It went down the drain, there." She waved at the water. "My phone, my iPhone is in it."

The frog looked at the drain and then back at the self-professed fairy-princess. A smile, if frogs can smile, curved its lips, and a small pink tongue shot out to wet its left eye before disappearing as quickly as it emerged.

"Quiet, and dry thy eyes and reapply thy magic colors. I shall fetch thine clutch, but what wilt thou do for me in return?"

Knowing what all men lust for when they look upon her, she promised a kiss, for she had surely kissed far worse looking men than this frog.

Upon hearing the offered reward, the creature took a deep breath and was gone. Only to moments later, reappear with the rhinestone clutch in its mouth. Slowly, it swam closer. When it was only inches from where she sat in the shallow pool, it stood on its hind legs, took the clutch from his mouth, and handed it over.

She took the clutch and opened it. The contents were miraculously dry. She grabbed her phone and reflexively thumbed through her apps, checking the status of her girlfriends, as she had suspected, each of them had paired off for the night with some fine and well-cut man. All seeming good and right in the world, she dried the outside of the clutch, put her phone away. The music was still good, so she started to sway to the beat, until she felt a cold sticky hand on her leg. She looked down.

The frog looked up. Its lips, if frogs had lips to pucker, were ready to accept the offered reward.

"Fulfill thy promise."

She shivered. Suddenly, now that she had her clutch, she was disgusted by the creatures' slick green-brown visage and bulbous eyes that seemed to look everywhere at once.

"No."

She kicked at the creature. Her bare foot connected and sent it over the edge, but just before it went over, its tongue shot out from its mouth and opened a small wound upon her leg. When it landed on the ground, the creature was gone. In its place, on the floor below the stage, was a naked man about the self-professed fairy-princess' age.

Such an occurrence, anywhere else, would have caused a great disturbance, but the club seemed to barely notice. The music didn't skip a beat and those on the dance floor kept their hands in the air.

The naked man stood, his lean muscled body rippling in the disco-light.

"Thy behavior is most appalling."

The music stopped. The club went dark. Seconds later, both the music and the light came back on with a renewed intensity, and the naked man was gone. In his place, the frog looked up with what could only be anger in its bulbous eyes. Then, it hopped into the crowd, disappearing.

Thinking nothing more about the incident, because it was not the strangest of visions she had seen while out clubbing, and promising herself to lay off the E and Coke, she resumed dancing. Suddenly, in the middle of another of her favorite anthems, she had the most curious craving. She got down off the center stage, and was quickly replaced by another such self-professed fairy-princess, and got herself to the bar where she gazed longingly at the worms in the various sized Tequila bottles.

As the shirtless bartender made his way over to take her drink order, she caught an ever so slight twitching in the air several feet above her head. Reflexively, her glossy pink lips parted, and in less time than it took her to bat her eyelashes flirtatiously to get the attention of the bartender, her tongue shot out, caught what was in the air, and retracted.

"What can I pour thee?"

Stepping back from the bar she flipped her hair, filling the space where she'd stood with a rainbow shimmer. Looking back over her shoulder, still standing tall in her heels, she caught a glimpse of her changing complexion in the mirror behind the bar and then in the ceiling. Her eyes were beginning to bulge, her lips thinning, her skin yellowing. She managed to keep her composure, even as she croaked out a burp. To her, it was part of just another night out on the town. Suddenly, she felt another urge.

"Oh, nothing. I just think I need a swim."

Then, she disappeared into the dancing crowd toward the aquarium of colorful and exotic frogs with an unrequited wish upon her lips.

Running of the Cows

My name will not be found in any bylines. I'm a ghostwriter for the New Mexico Chronicle big shots. I like it that way. Let the bigwigs sit in their offices and get fat putting their names on my work, just as long as I get to travel and witness news firsthand. I didn't go to Albuquerque Technical Institute to sit in some office, but I sure as hell didn't sign up for that. I don't care how much NMC pays me. I'm not going back there. I will not go back to the Wall. If they want this pen's ink, then they'll need to send it north for a spell, away from the Wall and away from Samuel Holt, poor damned soul. Sergeant Holt is gone as I see it; he's crazy. By all rights, I should be too.

See, the NMC wanted to do a series of human-interest stories about the men and women of the U.S. Border Patrol and Customs. They wanted some liberal story about how the CBP agents were not all racist Mexican killers, fascist white supremacists, or complete nut jobs that couldn't get a real job out of high school. I thought that if this was the story they needed, why not send one of their equal opportunity cabana boys. I'm sure that when the story prints tomorrow, it won't have my name under the title. Instead, it'll be Juanita Sanchez. Names don't really matter as long as I'm somewhere else tomorrow. Shit, send me to the Philmont Scout Ranch⬜ to cover a jamboree or relations between the Apache and the local ranchers. Just don't send me back to the Wall.

Samuel Holt's name was given to me by one of my contacts. He said that Holt had enough pull to get me into one of the towers. My contacts always pay out. This was no different. I met up with Holt at the Barracks, a local pub for the CBP and The Minuteman Civil Defense Corps. The owners hate Mexicans and anyone who's willing to voice a similar opinion gets their first round free. The place was typical: dark, smoky, with a long wooden bar that curved. The one standout was the plasma wall screen that everyone was parked in front of like a bunch of movie goers. Except that they were watching some amateur footage of a MCDC team round up a woman and a bunch of kids into a white van, their wrists tied with plastic garbage pulls. A guy with a yellow-stained mustache behind the bar cheered as one of the kids fell to his knees and cried out. The video had no sound. Instead, Johnny Cash was playing in the background.

I pulled up a barstool. The man with the yellow mustache finished cleaning a highball and put it in front of me. His eyes never left t he screen.

"What can I get you?"

"Water."

He looked at me. He had green eyes and the stains in his mustache were really blond patches. "If you're not drinking or smoking, Mister, you should leave."

"I'm with the New Mexico Chronicle."

"I don't remember asking." He poured two fingers of something pungent and brown into the glass. "That's ten."

I reached for my wallet. His shoulders relaxed. "I'm looking for Sergeant Holt." I waved the glass toward the crowd. "He here?"

"Holt," he bellowed.

A man of medium build in a white tank top, bigger than me for sure, muscled, short hair, and sharp eyes, turned around. He was younger than I expected. From what my contact told me, Holt had seen three tours in Iraq. Holt didn't look a day over twenty-two. He pulled a cap down low over his eyes.

I stuck my hand out. "I'm with the New Mexico Chronicle."

"Samuel." He took my hand.

I lifted my chin in the direction of the screen. "What's with all that?"

He shrugged.

My contact had said that Holt didn't like to talk and that he would not be a great source for commentary. He wasn't kidding.

"Okay, okay. How do you want to do this?" I put my drink down.

"You will ride in the back of my jeep."

"Good." Nothing. That was it. Holt took his drink and went back to his seat in the crowd.

I drank my drink and ordered a BLT with extra bacon and a side of ranch to go along with the second round the bartender poured when I emptied the first. This bar was like no other I'd been in. No one talked. They just watched the MCDC footage like worshipers at a backwoods revival. No one came in after me and no one left. It was like everyone that was anyone in these parts was here already, all joined in a single unity that I could not grasp.

Time passed. I had a few more, closing out my tab after each drink with the hope that Holt and I would leave. I ended up watching like everyone else. The soundless shaky camera coldly reported the finishing touches on the Wall. It ended with footage from the completion ceremony, the governor of New Mexico sliding the last brick into place in our segment of the wall and saluting the men and women who had signed on to patrol.

Then Holt was standing beside me. He looked at my bag. "I need to search that."

"Sure."

He picked it up and opened the flap. He pulled out my recorder and handed it to me along with my camera, video camera, and MP3 player. "You have a cell?"

I pulled it out of my pocket and held it up.

"Leave all this in your car."

I held up my hands. "What can I bring?"

"Everything else," He handed my bag back. "I hope you're not afraid of small enclosed places." Holt led me out back to his jeep. There was a long box in the back smaller than a coffin, but bigger than a hope chest. AMMO was written in block letters across the top. Holt opened the lid. "Get in."

The ride was uneventful. The road was a little bumpy and I questioned why I really needed a firsthand account of the CBP in action. I've taken liberties before when the circumstances were too unconventional, like the time I was asked to infiltrate a methamphetamine racket. I moved into a trailer for a week and watched as little girls lugged jugs and buckets back and forth between their homes and a large machine shed at the end of the road. I didn't really feel it was necessary to actually make the stuff to write about the process.

The jeep stopped. I was about ready to jump out when I heard voices.

"You got the overnight?"

"Yep."

"Lucky. The night watch sees all the action. What's your count?"

"Lost track."

"Bullshit. I heard you've got more than a hundred."

"Could be. I just point and shoot."

"Well tonight will be no different. We're under a code red tonight. No one's going to get much sleep, I think. Intel says there's going to be a rush."

"There's one every night. What's different?"

"Don't know. They say it's going to be bigger than Day 1."

"We'll see. Am I clear to go?"

"Oh, yeah. Sure, Sergeant. All clear."

The engine started up again and we drove for a while longer. My legs were beginning to ache, my bladder was full, and I was beginning to feel nauseous. I had better get a bonus for this one. Then again, at least I'm not embedded somewhere. Johns, a good friend of mine, was with the media corps in Iraq. He's still missing.

The car stopped again. I could hear the jeep door open and shut. Even in the box the air was drier here and there were strong metallic and oil smells. The back opened. Then the lid to my box creaked open.

"Wow, thanks."

Holt shined his flashlight out towards the wall. Well, fence really. It looked to be about thirty feet high. It had floodlights that illuminated the desert on the Mexican side. "We're up there." He flicked the beam of the light up at a watchtower that reminded me of some European castle turret, except with more of a machine shed look to it. The roof was angled to the right and left. A rope ladder hung to the ground. Holt then pointed out a latrine. "Hide." He took off with purpose toward the ladder.

I ducked behind the green port-a-potty. All this hiding was getting on my nerves. My next assignment better be those Boy Scouts or the sanitary union strike in Los Lunas. It smelled like the port-a-potty hadn't been emptied in a few days and had cooked in the sun. All of a sudden, I really didn't need to use it.

I could hear a door open and shut. The jeep started and drove off. I stepped out from behind the latrine to see the red glow of tail lights disappearing into the night. Had Holt left me here? Some joke. I didn't really think Holt the joking kind. It must have been the change in watch.

A light blinded me. It came from the door in the watch tower. I ran over to the ladder and climbed up. "I thought that..."

Holt had his finger over his lips. He pointed to a camera and tapped his ears. He handed me a piece of paper. The note read:

Keep quiet. Sit in the corner. Camera can't see you there. Microphones.

I took the seat. I looked around as Holt moved from a laptop in the center of a metal folding table, to a large computer terminal near the killslot, a slit in the wall facing south. The killslot was six feet long and two feet tall. The terminal's monitor displayed a cockpit, complete with crosshairs and elevation and distance markers. The screen moved slowly as Holt used the track ball mouse to position the General Dynamics 12.7mm, .50 caliber, XM312 Machinegun. I'd never seen one up close. If CBP had these every 300 yards from San Diego to the Gulf of Mexico near Palo Alto, they could conceivably operate the border from anywhere in the world.

Except for the machinegun and its controls, the table, the laptop, my chair, and Holt's ergonomic office chair, the room was completely empty. The walls were bare except for a large map of the border with red dots. It looked like a subway route, each dot a stop. One of the dots was green. It was in New Mexico, so I assumed that it was our location.

Holt made some adjustments to the machinegun and logged something on the laptop. He then pulled a deck of cards and a pack of cigarettes out of his bag and placed them on the table. He lit up as he spread the cards out for a game of solitaire.

It was going to be a long night. Holt had told me to leave all my electronics behind. I just had a pen and my notepad. I watched Holt lose a couple of games. He stopped about mid-game each time to adjust the machinegun and log information on the laptop. I decided to make a few notes for my article:

Atmosphere of complete boredom
Scent of gun oil and stale smoke
The rapid fire of shuffling playing cards echoed off bare walls
Eerie green glow of monitor
Hot, sweat, no AC
50 yards of mined sand stretches between us and them
Box of coiled destruction nestled underfoot

Loneliness

Red light flashes, whining alarm sounds

Holt left the cards where they lay on the table and rolled his chair over to the terminal. He stubbed out his cigarette. The monitor swiveled. There were red dots like space invaders hovering at the top of the screen.

"Sanders, Levine, confirm heat signatures on my Twelve."

"Confirmed."

"Confirmed, Holt. I got at least 50 between my 9 and your 12."

Holt left the monitor and used binoculars. "Control, come in Control."

"Control. Go ahead."

"Control, this is Holt NW 145. I have over 100 head of cattle nearing my sand trap. Please advise."

"Control authorizes code Stoplight. Use extreme caution. We now have a live feed. We see what you see."

Holt turned around and looked right at me. He put both of his hands on the seat of his chair and jerked up.

I did the same and nodded my head.

Holt swiveled around and placed his left hand on the keyboard and his right on the track ball.

"This is Control. We've determined that there is a mixture of heat signatures. Drones are vectoring now."

I watched as Holt brought up two small windows on his monitor. They displayed a high-resolution view of fast-moving ground from what must be more than a mile up; trees and buildings looked like small toys. The views slowed. The one on top first recorded a large herd of cattle milling about. The lower one caught a glimpse of several parked buses.

"This is Control. Threat confirmed. Dispatching Big Birds now. ETA 30 minutes."

Holt turned and looked at me. He wore an expression of worry mixed with glee. He crumpled pieces of paper to cover his voice. "When this shit hits, hide in the latrine. Stay out of sight." He tossed the paper aside.

I must have looked bad because Holt smiled warmly to reassure me that it would be alright.

"This is Control. Sanders, Holt, Levine, sound off."

"This is Sanders. I have the 3. This is going to be messy. When I was in 'nam a buddy of mine...I'll just say we never did find his left leg."

"This is Holt. I got the 12. Sanders, you're one sick fuck."

"This is Control. Cut the side chatter."

"This is Levine. I've got the 9."

"This is Control. They're going to try to concentrate the stampede to clear the mines, don't fire until they cross on to U.S. soil. Try to cut down as many as you can and divert the herd."

In the distance, I could hear the bus horns honk like a thousand angry geese. The red dots on Holt's monitor moved into range, becoming distinct cow shapes. Now, I've been around cows. They're not smart, but I just didn't think it was possible.

Holt yelled, "My 10, my 10." Holt held down a key with this left hand and the machinegun rocked into action. The sound was deafening, like golf ball sized hail on a metal roof.

The scent of hot oil filled my nose. I stood and moved to the door. I watched the monitor. The herd panicked, running on adrenaline. I could see that Holt and the others were making direct hits, but the crazed cows kept coming. A couple dropped and the herd swerved a few feet and kept coming. Then the one in the lead hit a mine and thunder erupted from the ground, hurling the carcass in every direction. The stampede charged through to the next mine and then another. *Boom, Boom, Boom.* The air filled with the stench of burning flesh. But the stampede kept charging.

Holt worked the track ball like a champion Centipede player. He was completely focused.

"They're going to get through. They're going to hit the wall," someone yelled.

It was time to leave. I opened the door and started down the ladder. Halfway down, the wall shook like a tank hit it. I lost my grip and fell to the ground. I quickly rebounded and ran for the latrine without looking back. It was the only object for miles. I ducked behind it.

I heard cows screaming as the stampede slammed into the wall. I peeked around the side and saw large bodies hammering into one another, so scared that they were trampling one another. The wall moved. And it broke as the mad cattle pushed through. The flood lights in the immediate area blinked out. I held my knees against my chest as the stampede ran into the night, like a freight train off its tracks.

But the night's horrors were just starting. I watched headlights appear between the cracks in the wall. I heard the screams of people as one of the buses raced through. I could barely see it in the light of the moon, but what I could see, turned my stomach. The side of the bus was full of holes and one of the front tires wobbled until the bus flipped onto its side.

As the second bus made it through in similar condition, people were emptying out of the first and quickly limping in the darkness. I saw a mother carrying her baby in a basket drag her leg as she tried to hurry away.

Then I heard it. I heard what could only be the blades of helicopters. A floodlight turned night into day. A terrible sawing sound started as the helicopters' mini-guns cut the runners down. The other let a missile loose and the second bus left the ground and landed, broken and in flames.

I lowered myself onto the ground and like a snake disappeared into the sand. Wherever the helicopters' floodlights shined, the sand erupted as if a hard rain struck the ground. One of the helicopters disappeared over the Wall. The other kept sweeping back and forth.

That's when everything got real quiet. One of the helicopter landed as a bunch of jeeps pulled up. I knew that I was busted at that point. So, I stood up, put my hands behind my head and thanked God that I was a man of average height and white as I walked in to the open.

The First Supper

In a large room with a long table and high back chairs, at the edge of the galaxy known only to its indigenous species as the Milky Way, a lavish dinner had only just started. The room was sterile. The walls hung no adornments. The floor was a single sheet of rock or steel, either way, it was seamless and a neutral gray cool, matching the wall, table, and chairs. The room looked as if it had simply carved itself from the asteroid's surface. And perhaps it had. The room's non-existent décor was intentional, a way to accentuate the beauty of the dinner guests, some of whom were still arriving.

The doorman stood at the ready, a tall fellow with multiple appendages branching from his torso. He had so many such appendages that if he had a head (not everyone has a head you must know), it must have been smallish and unimportant. As each new arrival entered, the doorman would quickly snatch the guest's outer garments. Next, the doorman would announce the guest's name (if the guest had one), home plant, and position or status. These events were rarely ever attended by a non-dignitary. The common classes usually didn't possess the money or pallet necessary to appreciate a treat such as this one.

"Tal Ringdancer. York-9. Highness – Crown Wearer," the doorman trumpeted, causing everyone to turn and bow. Whispers quickly floated around the room.

"Dinner must be special to bring out a Crown Wearer."

"What's so special about this meal?"

"I don't care if he's a Crown Wearer. I'm not going to watch my language – the prissy cunt."

"Quiet. You don't want to offend a Crown Wearer. The last being to have caused offence ended up on the menu."

"There goes the evening."

And such were the utterances caused by the surprise appearance of a Crown Wearer, the ruling class of all that is known to exist. The Crown Wearer classes were old, and Tal was older than most. The orange skin showing through between the edges of his loose fitting robes was starting to green as if mold had attacked the rind of a Terran's mandarin. The edges of his eyes were rutted so deeply that they threatened to envelope his vision. If he'd had hair, he'd lost it long ago. Besides wrinkles around his eyes and lips, he was slick and perfectly smooth.

He addressed the crowd, "Guests." He paused breathing deeply in through his mouth, inflating like a balloon, before continuing. "I am here not as guest but as opportunity provider. Your meal today, if you like, has potential investment opportunity. Once you have eaten, instead of your normal resource payments, I only require a few standard units of your time." Out of breath, he returned to his normal shape and size. Then, he moved to the head of the table and sat down as the whispers exchanged a few quick words.

"I knew it."

"A bloody sales pitch, from a Crown Wearer no less."

"Can I say no? Dare I?"

"This better be damn good, or I'll..."

"Quiet!"

"I just want to eat."

Tal clapped. Where there were no doors, doors opened and a server for each guest entered carrying lidded trays. The room was suddenly filled with strong scents of breaded meats fried in oil. The aroma was almost too much for a few of the guests to withstand.

One guest, a smallish creature – mostly mouth and teeth – jumped up onto the table. Its round body quivered on its three stool-like legs. It hopped up and down for a second before turning to see that every other creature had turned from the servers to look directly at it. "What?" It asked. "I've been fasting for almost a full cycle." Then, because it could see that the servers were waiting for it to get down from the table, it hopped backed into its chair.

Tal clapped, again. This time, what must have been the chef emerged in a white breasted coat and a tall white hat. The creature was thin, purple, and smelled of sandy beaches covered in dead fish. It opened only one of its mouths to say, "Before you" – the servers placed the dishes on the table – "you have a lightly breaded selection of phalanges upon toasted pine nuts. As you can see around the outside of your plate, you have two types of dipping sauces that complement the dish well: one is tangy and sweet while the other is tart and hot. Please, allow me to demonstrate how they are eaten."

The server standing behind the chef opened a tray. The chef picked one of the phalanges and dipped it in the hot sauce. Next, he opened his mouth wide and his lips wider. He placed the phalanges just inside his mouth before cutting through the bread and meat with his teeth. He then twisted the phalange around and pulled the meat away, leaving a completely white multi-jointed bone.

"You see," said the chef. "You eat the meat, but you do not eat the bone."

The guests turned to look at their plates as the chef, the servers, and the doors in the room disappeared.

"Not much meat here."

"What? Am I expected to eat this – this filler? Bring on the main course."

"Yeah! I'm hungry."

"What's the big deal?"

Tal stood. He looked out over the guests and everyone quieted down. He then sat back down while saying, "Remember two things: one, I am here…"

"How could we forget?"

"Yeah. The destroyer of fun."

"…two," Tall continued, "I'm paying for this meal, so I expect some civility." Showing his frustration with the lower classes, he also added, "Tonight's meal will be served in courses. Calm, please." He leaned back in his chair and ate his phalanges one by one. When he was finished, he clapped again.

The doors opened, again. This time two servers for every guest emerged: one to quickly remove finished plates and the other to set the next dish. When the lids were removed the rich aroma of a bone marrow broth and herbs caused several of the guests to drool. The chef described the dish as a femur or thigh bone reduction with thigh and calf meat.

"More like it."

"Wonderful flavor."

"So tender. It must have cooked for hours."

"The vegetables, precisely cut and just the right firmness."

"Vegetables?"

"Yeah. I like the way they feel on my tongue."

"I just eat around those things. To biter. Besides, I want to leave more room for the good stuff."

"The meat?"

"Yes! Meat!"

When Tal had finished his soup, he didn't check to see if the others had finished. Instead, he clapped and bowls were removed and large plate set in their place.

The chef explained the new dish, which smelled of wood and hot fat, "Another finger food. This one is covered in a rich honey glaze and was smoked until tender. The meet is best removed with your teeth, just as you did with the phalanges."

One guest, the creature that had jumped on the table unable to control its original excitement, squealed and took one of the long glazed ribs in its small thick hand. It put the entire rib into his mouth and quickly cleaned it. "My goodness..." It fell back into its chair. "Is this species abundant? How can so many flavors and textures come from one creature?"

Tal took that opportune moment as an introduction. He stood. "Keep eating. Our little hungry blue friend from the P'lg system has provided me a moment to speculate with you."

The far wall disappeared revealing a large cage. The cage was wheeled closer to the tables and contained three large bi-pedal mammals, two male and one female. The mammals were awake and seemed to be attempting some kind of communication with one another, but whatever vocalizations they were attempting sounded like nothing more than guttural intake and exhalation of air. The two males moved in front of the female. Naked, the males seemed to hold the attention of the guests more than the female anyway, so there was no need to rearrange them for display.

Tal moved in front of the cage. He was taller than the cage but as wide. Still, one of the guests politely asked him to move aside, which he did with as much of a smile as a Crown Wear could muster when asked to do anything. Thus, standing to the side of the cage so as not to obscure any the guests' view, Tal began his sales pitch.

"Opportunity." He paused. "Opportunity stands before you in this cage. This species is plentiful and, as you have tasted, delicious when prepared properly."

One of the guests, a slender pink reedy looking fellow, interrupted. "I'm eating here. Make it quick. Get to the point."

The rest of guests, if they had necks, looked to suffer from whiplash. Their heads snapped from Tal to the pink fellow and back to Tal. Interrupting the speech of Crown Wearer was unadvisable at bests of times. There were rumors that the last individual to interrupt a Crown Wearer was sentenced to hard labor collecting gas from a ringed planet in this very system. Gas collection was an occupation with the life expectancy of less than two full cycles. However, the interruption seemed to give confidence to other guests.

"Yeah. Be quick."

"More food."

Instead of reprimanding the guests, Tal simply continued. "Investment. Even I do not have the funds to move on this opportunity. Thus, I need you to consider investment." He paused.

"What this?"

"You want more of our money?"

"Aren't the levies enough?"

Tal held up his hand. "You misinterpret my intentions. Investment, not tax. This venture is not Crown Wearer sanctioned. This is business." To make his point, Tal removed the crown from his head. He held it out for one of his servants hold. "I use not funds collected, but my funds earned."

The guests were silent. Even the blue creature that was mostly mouth had stopped eating. Not one of them had ever seen a Crown Wearer remove his or her crown. It was a symbol of authority, position, and power. To give up that power was unheard of.

"So, what do you want? Be clear."

"Yes. Clear."

Tal pointed at the creatures in the cage. "My people invested in the third planet from this system's sun long ago. We planted these creatures there, except they were smaller, and they had more hair cover, thicker hides, etc. Just last cycle, I discovered documents, long lost, that told of this planet and a plan to grow a harvest like none ever recorded. I sought out the planet and found populations beyond wildest predictions. The harvest is ready, but I alone, by myself, lack the means. I come to you asking investment for a return in the profit."

"What does that mean? Be clearer."

Tal snapped. The sound echoed in the room. Then the bipeds were rolled out of the room and an image of the local solar system appeared in the vacated space between the wall and the guests. Tal walked into the image. As he talked and pointed, new images appeared as if he were building a model.

"Here is where we would construct a gate. From the gate, all our systems would be accessible. Here," he pointed to a moon around a gas giant, "is where we would split shares and conduct sales."

"How many of them are there? How quickly do they mature?"

"Are they difficult to harvest? They look capable?"

"All good questions," said Tal. "They are very capable, which is why weren't not going to setup on their home world. I won't lie to you. There will be losses on our side. However, there are currently six and half billion of them, and my projections put them at nine billion in forty of their cycles. Mature stock takes twenty cycles. However, we must act quickly. They threaten themselves by not controlling their numbers and degrading their ecological resources. If we don't cull the herd soon, we might see their populations crash in sixty or seventy of their cycles."

"No good. "

"Not good."

"The tasties must survive."

"I agree," Tal sucked in more air and nodded. "They also suffer from some minor diseases, and some from malnutrition, and some from extreme overnutrition. If we involve our selves, we will be able to perfect the species – *the tasties* – in less than one hundred of their cycles. Yet, the urgent matter before us is capital investment, marketing, and the development of systems to insure sustainable production."

Tal waved his hand and the image of the local solar system disappeared. "For those interested, after we have eaten our fill, I would like to set a date for a further round of discussions. But for now, I have a treat to present."

Tal clapped. The doors open and the servers rushed in removing empty platters and placing one large dish in the center of the table. When all but one of the servers had exited, the remaining server removed to lid revealing a smaller version of the biped species. It's head was turned to the side, it's skin was a glazed and golden brown, and it was nestled on top of a bed of greens. A large red fruit was stuffed in its mouth. The aroma was heavenly.

"I'm in." Was echoed loudly and by everyone in the room as they picked up various utensils.

Tal took his seat and smiled a wide grin that showcased a mouth full of sharp, white, and jagged teeth. "Eat. Eat. We'll discuss business later."

The Return of *Melanoplus spretus*

Dark Cloud Horizon

Jim stood in the potato field with a hand full of dirt. His father had sent him out to check the ground for early frost, which Jim had known to be a fool's errand. Yes, Jim knew that a deep frost would ruin the Russets, but he also knew that it was too early in the season for frost. His father should have said to check for blight or beetles, especially beetles.

This time of year, the *Leptinotarsa decemlineata* were everywhere. Not too many people used incest's Latin names, but Jim's father though a thing should be called by its proper binomial, or genus and species, name. Jim thought his father was a little daft and needed to sound smart around the other farmers. Jim's father had given up on teaching science to kids Jim's age, so they moved out of the city and bought a small farm in Idaho.

Jim's father had no intention of trying to compete with the other farms in the area. Instead, they grew several varieties of potato, just enough to sell locally to restaurants and at farmer's markets that wanted a pesticide-free, low impact product. Growing potatoes without the aid of big machines and large quantities of chemicals seemed impossible to the neighboring farmers, and when they saw Jim's father around the way, they called him names. Once, Mr. Orson spit on Jim's father's shoes while they were in the grocery store picking up diapers and formula for Jim's baby sister.

Jim had begged his father several times to call a Colorado potato beetle a Colorado potato beetle instead of *Leptinotarsa decemlineata* and a potato a potato instead of *Solanum tuberosum*, but there was no changing his father. Most days, Jim admired his father's use of names. However, Jim's father's stubbornness was starting to wear Jim down. Jim was tried of defending his father's quirks.

After checking the soil, Jim walked the rows of purple flowers. He'd stop every ten yards, cup the flowers and inspect the sun-yellow stamens, turn a few of the leaves over, and shake the plant. When he shook the plant, a few light green short-horned grasshoppers fell to the ground. Jim scooped one up in his hand, "*Melanoplus sanguinipes*. No wings, yet. You can't get far then." Jim liked seeing grasshoppers in the fields because if their populations were high then there wouldn't be a large, and thus uncontrollable, infestation of the Colorado potato beetle. The Colorado potato beetle laid its eggs near grasshopper's eggs. The Colorado potato beetle usually hatched first, and its larva would eat grasshopper eggs, one pest controlling the population of the other. However, a potato farmer hates both, but Jim's father saw opportunity in grasshoppers where the Colorado potato beetle only brought devastation. Jim and his father would catch grasshoppers and sell them to high-end restaurants in Denver. Potato beetles were inedible, simply a pest.

Jim held on to the pair, putting them in a small glass jar with tiny air holes in the plastic lid. Jim pulled a leaf from a near by plant and stuffed it in the jar along with the captive bugs. His father would want to see the pair for himself. He put the jar in his side-satchel and looked back up at the house.

The lights were on in only one room, his parents. Jim had know they'd wanted a little alone time, wanted him out of the house for a while so they could do what adults did while they were alone. Many of Jim's friends' parents were divorced, separated, or seemed to loath each other. He didn't know what was different about his parents, but Jim was mature enough to know that his parents were still attracted to each other. Now, while Jim didn't think on his parents' sex life for very long, because like any good teenager, he found it gross, he was glad they still had sex – that they were still together.

Jim spun around. He swore he could hear buzzing. A loud raspy buzzing had suddenly risen with the sun's setting. With the sun at its zenith, Jim pulled out his flashlight. He pointed the flashlight's beam in the air as he swatted around his head. The buzzing stopped and the sun was again bright, but Jim was left with a gut wrenching feeling that some trouble had just passed by overhead.

Not waiting around to see if whatever had buzzed his head would come back, Jim took off for the house. When he pulled the porch door open, Jim called out, "Father! There's something in the field."

Jim's father, shirtless, pulling up his pants, came running into the living room. "What's out there?" Jim's father waited barely a second. "Come on, Jimmy. What's going on?"

"I heard a buzzing." Jimmy made the motions of swatting over his head. "But I couldn't see nothing 'cause the sun had gone out."

" 'Anything'. You couldn't see anything."

"Right. I couldn't."

"And you heard buzzing. What kind of buzzing?" Jim father was pulling on a long sleeved red and brown flannel.

"Like mosquitoes but bigger." As Jimmy tried to explain that the buzzing had come from everywhere, as illustration to his story, a light tink-tink plus a mosquito like buzzing emanated from his satchel. Jim stopped mid-sentence and pulled the jar out of his bag. "Yeah, father. Like this."

Jim's father took the jar and opened it. He turned the jar upside down and shook it. A brown grasshopper fell into his hand. Jim father held it out to Jim. "Son, this is very important. What color was this *Melanoplus* when you put it in the jar?"

"Green."

Jim father walked out onto the porch with he bug in his left hand and the jar in his right. "It's not possible." He looked again at the sample his son had brought him from the field. "Jim, I have one more question for you." He held the grasshopper out for Jim to see. "You see any other difference?"

Jim took the grasshopper between his thumb and his two middle fingers. "Sure father. This one has wings."

Then Jim's father said, "Quiet. Listen."

Jim listened. From seemingly all around, Jim could hear a grinding, chewing noise. "What's that?"

Jim's father walked though the clean cut grass yard to the edge of the field. On his way, he stopped and picked up a butterfly net that was lying in his path. They used the nets to catch beetles before squishing them. However, he stopped at the edge of the yard and the field. Standing in the early evening sun, Jim's father watched his field of Russets undulate like high tide, waves of brown and yellow ebbed and slapped at his feet.

The tide looked like the soil had gotten fed up with providing the water and some of the nutrients necessary to grow a thick tuber of sugary starch and was revolting. Jim's father took the butterfly net, angled it against the tide, and scooped up a net full of grasshoppers identical to the one he pulled from Jim's bottle.

Having separated the net full of grasshoppers from the tide, a harsh ear crushing buzzing erupted from the ocean before him. Quickly, he rejoined the netted grasshoppers with those in his field. The buzzing stopped, replaced with the chewing sound.

Jim had sunk up on his father. He stood next to where his father had emptied the net back into the field. "Why did you toss'em back?"

"Not now." Jim's father said. "We need to slowly make our way back to the house."

"What are they?"

"*Melanoplus spretus*." He took his teenaged son's hand. "Back up slowly."

Jim shook his father's hand. He hadn't held his father's hand since he started playing football in the sixth grade. His father's hand had felt wet and limp. He didn't want to hold that hand. He'd always believed that his farther was strong and fearless, but that hand had conveyed the opposite. At that moment, he stopped thinking of the man slowly backing up the yard to the house as his father. Instead, he only saw a man named Galvin.

Jim thought, "I'm not afraid of no grasshopper, no matter the species name." Aloud he said, "I'm not going to let them take our crop," before running toward the field.

"James." Jim's father called. "James, no! Those are Rocky Mountain Locusts."

Jim charged ahead into the tidal wave of locusts. As Jim's shoes crunched and squished the invertebrates' exoskeletons, the insects seemed to pull away, parting as Moses had parted the Red Sea. However, Jim did not have a watchful, loving God looking out for him at that moment. As the tide of locusts parted, they piled atop one another creating ten-foot columns forming a perfect three-dimensional horseshoe. The horseshoe opened back toward the yard.

Jim's father called out repeatedly. His words of warning swallowed by agitated buzzing and chewing. He ran to the porch, slung the garden hose over his shoulder, and headed back down toward the field. However, as he turned around, after hefting the hose over his shoulder and tuning on the water, his son and the horseshoe of locusts had been claimed by the plague.

Plague Moving

Galvin wasn't going to give up on his son. James could still be alive, buried under a mountain of insects. Putting his thumb over the end of the garden hose, he focused the water pressure where he thought he'd last seen James stomping, trying to protect their meager harvest of *Solanum tuberosum*. Just then, while spraying the field, he thought "Potatoes. They're potatoes."

"James." He yelled. He changed direction with the stream of water. A small rainbow appeared in the spray as the sun sunk even lower on the horizon. As the water pushed the plague back, he caught sight of his son's shoe.

He doubled his efforts, tying to get more force out of the hose.

Suddenly, besides his frantic efforts with the garden hose, the chewing and buzzing stopped. A deafening quiet over took the field. The tidal motion ceased, but the insects were still everywhere, covering everything as far as he could see.

Then, just as suddenly as the plague had stopped moving and buzzing, it exploded off the ground. A dark cloud choked out what light was left from the sun. For the next several minutes, the thunder of the locusts' movement caused Galvin to drop the hose and forget about his son, as his own flight instincts tried to protect him.

He fell to his knees first. He then curled as tightly as he could into the fetal positing, trying to cover his face. His efforts weren't enough to save him from the extreme weight of the insects as they all tried to get airborne at once. If he hadn't been holding his breath and squirming around, he would have compared the bombardment to suffocation he'd only heard about when someone got trapped in a grain elevator. It was never the weight that killed, but either panic or the inhalation of dust – like drowning in dirt instead of water.

As Galvin gasped for air, he pulled his chin under his shirt and took a breath through the fabric. Being able to take that breath calmed his nerves enough to remember that his son was still trapped in the field. However, he could do nothing other than wait for the plague to pass.

While he waited, the stress pushed his mind into a stupor of connections. *Names*. He'd always believed that names possessed a spiritual power unlike any other facet of human nature. Names, he believed, were divine in origin. First, God created and named man and woman, naming them Adam and Eve. In the joy that God took from creating and naming everything in the universe, God found joy watching Adam and Eve, together, as they discovered each of those names.

Galvin asked his fear laced brain, why would God bring back an insect extinct since 1902? Galvin fought against the idea and sought other answers. There was another grasshopper close in DNA structure, the *Melanoplus bruneri* – largest of the North American Grasshoppers still in existence. However, the *Melanoplus bruneri* lived a more solitary life, only gathering in small clusters to find mates. They'd never swarmed liked the Rocky Mountain Locusts made famous by Laura Ingalls Wilder and Rose Wilder Lane's story, "On the Banks of Plum Creek." Still, the only difference between a grasshopper and a locust, which was only scientific speculation, was behavior. While the grasshopper lived solitarily, the locust was gregarious – clustering and moving en masse.

None of those thoughts eased the panic that Galvin felt as he waited for the plague to lift. As his thoughts cleared, he risked peaking out from under his flannel shirt. The plague was gone, save for a littler of casualties scattered over the lawn. Uncurling, he carefully got to his feet.

Before he could check on his son, his wife had run past into the field. For a second, he wondered how much she had seen from the house. How helpless she must have felt watching the cloud of insects first envelop her son and then her husband. He picked up the garden hose and put it over his shoulder. Then he ran after his wife into the field.

"June. June." He called.

June looked up. She held a tattered shirt and one shoe. "Where is he?"

Galvin looked around in the dark. The moon's light was strong tonight, but he could barely see anything. Searching, he tripped over something. Fumbling in the dark, he took hold of what he'd tripped over.

Bone. He held a bone in his hand. Summoning all his naming strength, he dispassionately named them *radius* and *ulna*, the two bones that composed the human forearm. The forearm was missing connective the tissue necessary to hold the two bones together or connect them to the *carpals* and *humerus*. He tried to find comfort in knowing those names, find the power, the connection to the divine.

North America, for the past hundred years, had the only been the only one of the six insect habitable continents to have successfully defeated a species of locust. Its sudden return was an affront to American agricultural dominance. Looking out over his fields with his son's *radius* and *ulna* in his right hand and the garden hose in his left, he cried out.

June stopped her search and ran over. She took the bones from his hand, the *radius* in her left and the *ulna* in her right, and hugged them to her chest. She fell to her knees. In the dirt, she swept her arms wide collecting more of her son to her.

Galvin sat. The garden hose still spewing water into the barren field. His next thought was mistakenly said aloud, "They took my son.

They took my plants, but we'll still have potatoes in the ground tomorrow."

June, not thinking, raised James' *radius* over her head hit Galvin square on the shoulder with it. Recognizing what she'd done, she dropped the bones and ran for the house.

Galvin couldn't find the power to move. He dug his fingers deep into the soil where his son had died. For several minutes, he dug with only one hand. Then giving into the act, he got to his knees and dug with both hands until he found a patch of small Russet tubers.

The tubers were small, about the size of his thumb. As he piled them, he couldn't help but think they wouldn't catch a good price at the farmer's market, and he likely go bankrupt trying to pay back the loan on the land and this season's seed spuds.

The pile he'd made contained more than a hundred fingerling sized Russets, and the hole in his field slightly short then he was tall and half a foot deep. He collected his son's bones and put them in the shallow grave before pushing the dug up soil back into the hole, over his son.

He took a moment before walking back to house. "Son," he said, "I'm not one to believe that you can hear me, but I was proud of you." A tear cleared a way down his dusty cheek. "You're last thoughts and actions were in the best interest of the farm, the family. You tried you best to salvage the crop. Tonight, son, you were your dad's hero."

He tossed a couple of potatoes on the grave that he'd been rolling around in his hand, he turned to walk back up the house to see about

June and his daughter Sarah-Beth.

Recovering

June watched Galvin walk in the door and sit down at the diner table. He took his shoes off, like he did every time he came in from the field, grunting and tired. He threw them next to the door.

Ignoring Galvin, June made another phone call. While her husband played in the dirt, she'd fired up the prayer chain. She'd stared with LuAnn, told her that the wrath of God had finally stuck her family because of her husband lack of faith and taken their son. She'd also relayed what she'd seen, trapped in the house.

"Susan. Heaven help me, I'm glad you answered. Don't go outside."

"What are you talking about, June? We were just about to go for our evening walk when I heard the phone ring.

"You can't."

"Well why not?"

"God's wrath just took James from us in a cloud of insects."

"Now June, tell me what you mean."

"I said it. My James is dead. I watched God's plague, just as it was in Egypt, come down out of the sky and kill my James."

"June."

"It's true. Don't go outside tonight. The Devil's loose. If you don't believe me, turn on the set, bound to be all over the news by now."

"Anyway, I need you to call the rest on the hotline. We need your prayers, and tell people to turn on the TV and stay inside to night."

"June, are you okay. Should I drive over?"

"No. Make the calls Susan." Before June heard Susan's answer, she hung up and dialed the next number on her list.

"May, you have to believe me. Turn on the TV. It's got to be on the TV by now." While June talked to May, the conversation going about as well as the others, she got up of the chair and turned on her own TV. She'd expected breaking coverage on every channel, but as she flipped, the nightly news coverage was the same as always: Weather, Sports, Politics. There was nothing about the end of the world or a death cloud of flesh eating insects.

June cut her conversation with May short. After disconnecting the line, she turned again to Galvin. Galvin was still sitting on the kitchen chair staring at his feet. "Gal, you have to warn people. Help me warn people."

"If it's not on the news already, it's too late." June marched over to where Galvin was sitting. She thrust the phone in his face. "Call."

"Who?"

"I don't know. Call the police, call the news, call your friends back at the university but heaven help me, you need to tell someone. You know what those were better than anyone, so it falls to you." She waved the phone under his chin until he took it.

"Okay." He said.

He dialed 911. He told the operator that his son was dead, and he'd buried him in the field with the potatoes. He used the word potato. When the operator had asked him what happened, he'd said he didn't know, only one moment he was alive and the next dead. The operator told Galvin to stay on the line and that emergency responders were being dispatched to their home. He'd said that he needed to make another call and hung up on the 911 dispatcher.

He called his friend Bill Reed next.

Bill answered on the third ring, "This is Bill."

"Bill, its Gal."

"Gal, it's getting late."

"Sorry about that, but my son is dead."

"What? What's that about James. Dead?"   "Dead."

"But how?"

"*Melanoplus spretus.*"

"Galvin, that's impossible. Even if the science was wrong and they still existed, The Rocky Mountain Locust didn't eat people. They only ate leaves and stalks, going have the dense sugars."

"It was them. I have samples."

"Okay, say I believe that you saw a swarm of grasshoppers. What direction they go?"

"East. Southeast, I think."

"I'll call in your warning, Gal. Wouldn't want people round here thinking that the Department of Agriculture didn't take a pest scare seriously." There was a pause. "But I'll check it out in the morning."

"Thanks."

"Sure thing."

They hung up.

Galvin turned to June. "I called." He stood, dropped the phone, walked down the hall, and went into James' room.

June followed Galvin. She'd heard only his end of the conversations and needed to know what was what. However, seeing Galvin sitting on the edge of James' bed clutching James' football jersey to his chest, stopped her short.

After a few moments, she got her nerve back and asked, "What?"

"What? What?"

"Who'd you call? What'd they say? You know, *what?*"

"The cops are on their way."

"Gal, what are the cops going to do about God's plague? Damn it man. You're the name guy. Power in names and all that. Do something."

"James is dead." He held up James' football helmet and shook it at June. "Dead.

"Our son is dead."

"The last reported swarm or plague of *Melanoplus spretus* occurred in late 1800's, perhaps as late as 1877." He went on as if reading out of a book. "It had been reported that the swarm contained nearly a trillion insects. No one knows why individual grasshoppers swarm becoming a plague of locusts. However, there has been speculation that *Melanoplus spretus*' life-cycle includes both a solitary phase and a..."

"Galvin." June slapped him, hard across the face.

He turned his head with the slap and dropped both James's helmet and jersey.

"You have to help save other folks' kids." She wound up as if to slap him again.

However, before June brought her hand down on Galvin's already red and swollen cheek, he stood. "What can I do?" Then he tore out of the house.

Aaron M. Wilson

Sending Them Back

Galvin pulled out of the parking lot and turned left. In his rearview mirror, he could see the flashing light of emergency vehicles turning off the highway and on the dirt road that ran past his home. He had an idea and didn't have time to discuss it with the police, especially since they'd suspect him of wrongdoing. He didn't have the kind of time necessary to explain that what took his boy also took his crop.

He sped down the road three driveways, until he came across Darrel's farm. Galvin pulled right up to Darrel's porch. His stop was more like a skid that threatened to take out a corner of the porch. Having barely come to a full stop, Galvin laid into the horn.

Darrel opened the door shielding his eyes from Galvin's high-beam lights.

Galvin got out of the truck and said, "We need your plane."

"What for?"

Instead of trying to talk it out, Galvin grabbed hold of Darrel and drug him off the porch and over to his field, which was no small feat. Darrel was a big man, standing over six feet and the size of Viking's linebacker. However, Galvin's surprise visit had caught Darrel off guard.

"Look," Galvin said.

The field was bare soil where five-foot tall corn stalks had been earlier that day. In the light from the house and Galvin's truck, small dust devils danced in the open field. The desolation of a season's work was utterly complete.

Galvin didn't want to explain about his son and the grasshoppers becoming a plague of *Melanoplus spretus*. He doubted that Darrel would believe him. Instead, he reached down and picked up a couple of specimens, handed them over to Darrel, and said, "We have to try."

Darrel held the critters in his hand, poked them with a chubby finger. Before pivoting on his heels, squishing the insects in his hand, he said, "We kill'em all."

They walked to the crop duster's hanger. Darrel went in through the door next to the large hanger door. Inside, he pressed the button to raise the large door so he could move his plane out of the hanger.

"Funny thing I just thought."

"What's that?"

"You, asking me for help."

"They killed James." Galvin said as he strapped the emergency parachute to his back. "They killed my son."

Darrel stopped his prep work and embraced Galvin. There was a quite moment between them. No slapping of backs as men do when the hug. Instead, a common resolve passed between them, so when they finally did let go of each other, Galvin's tears were wet on Darrel's shoulder, but Galvin's eyes were dry.

Darrel tossed Galvin a monkey wrench. "We need to get those tanks off."

They worked quickly. The takes were labeled with TOXIC and with the name of a pesticide company that Galvin didn't recognize. His tubers were organic, so he didn't spend time researching chemical companies. However, when Darrel handed over a new, full tank labeled DDT, he stopped.

"Gal, get that on."

"Wait. This stuff is bad news."

"You wanted to kill'em. This'll kill'em good."

"Yes, but..."

"But nothing. They took your son and my corn."

Galvin hoisted the tank into position and bolted it into place. Darrel was right. They needed to stop the plague tonight, not tomorrow, tonight. After affixing the tank, he tossed the wrench into the dirt and helped Darrel push the bi-wing out of the hanger.

"You ever flown this thing at night."

"Not supposed to, but yeah." Darrel grinned. "Come look."

Galvin crawled up the side and looked into the cockpit. "Wow."

"Yeah. I fixed my girl up with all the latest equipment." Darrel motioned for Galvin to get into the back seat. "She might look like the Red Baron flew her in the war, but she's a modern plane. Some of the pesticides require late night or early morning application because the sun breaks them darn too fast."

Galvin didn't have the chance to respond as the engine kicked over and the props sprang to life. Before he knew it, they were down the runway and in the air, heading East Southeast.

Without turning around, Darrel tapped his head, pointing to the headset and microphone.

Galvin found the equipment near his knees. He put the headset on, "Check, check, check."

"I can hear you, fine. You said east, yes."

"Yes."

"Good. They're flying into the wind, for now. If they head north, they'll catch the Jet stream."

Galvin imagined just how are they could make it if they gained the wind's help eastward. He remembered that reports of the locust plagues were recorded as far east and north as Maine, but the dustbowl states of Nebraska, Kansas, and Oklahoma were hit the worst in the last recorded swarm more than a hundred years ago.

"How are we going to spot them?"

"My girl's radar works like a fishing trawler, except for infestations of critters. If we fly over top'em, she'll spot'em."

The night air was cool and Galvin's face started to numb. He started to wish that he'd worn heavier clothes. Back on the ground, he wondered why Darrel had pulled on overalls and coat. Now he understood. The wind cut through the thin flannel shirt he wore.

Even though he was doing something, trying to help, sitting in the back seat of the plane, he felt helpless and alone. He knew that Darrel was up front. He watched as Darrel checked monitors hidden in the cockpit. How fast were the locusts? After what must have been thirty minutes of flying, Galvin started to wonder if he had imagined his son's death, the loss of his crop, and even being in the plane. The night's events seemed completely surreal.

A hard object struck Galvin in the face and fell in his lap. His first reaction was to put his hands up to shield his face from another pelting. Then he opened his eyes and saw the twitching body of a large brown grasshopper, a *Melanoplus spretus*.

Before Galvin could squish the bug, they flew into the cloud. The plane's props chopped hundreds of insects out of the air straining to keep the plane in the air.

"I think we found them." Darrel flicked a couple of switches and pull up for the sky. The switches released twin streams of DDT in their wake.

Galvin imagined what they must have looked like from the ground. A small bi-wing plane flying into a black cloud, and as the plane moved to crest over the cloud, like a waterfall, the black cloud fell to the ground.

"We got'em" yelled Darrel. "We got'em."

Aftermath

Galvin and Darrel stood next to the plane. The County Sheriff pointing his shotgun at the pair said, "What the hell boys?"

Darrel whooped it up. "Did you see that? We got'em. I think we got'em all." He spun around and slapped his knee.

The Sheriff cocked his shotgun. "Get in the back the car. Both of you." As Galvin walked by behind Darrel, the Sheriff grabbed hold of Galvin and pushed him up against his squad car. "Galvin, you're under arrest for the murder of your son James."

Galvin looked at the ground and let the Sheriff cuff him.

"Ken, we just saved Idaho." Darrel thought about what they'd done again and said, "No. We just saved the United States of America, maybe even some of Canada. We're heroes. Heroes don't get arrested." He swayed back and forth a bit.

"Darrel don't make me arrest you too. Wait, you been drinking and flying at night again? I've warned you." The Sheriff turned Galvin around and read him his Miranda rights."

"Quiet. Heroes aren't quiet." Darrel clapped his hands.

Galvin said. "Darrel, stop it."

"Tell'em what we did, tell'em."

"The Sheriff's going to take me down to the station and we'll talk it out. Do me a favor Darrel, tell June where I at." Galvin, without the help of the Sheriff, got into the back of the squad car.

"Wait. Wait." Darrel hand up his hand and ran out into the field.

The Sheriff looked to Galvin. "Darrel okay?"

"Sure."

"He's acting drunk again. He drunk?"

"I wouldn't know." Galvin suddenly realized how that sounded. "No. He's not drunk. He's right though."

"About you two saving the US?"

"I think so, yeah."

"From what?"

Galvin didn't reply. Instead, he lifted his chin to indicate Darrel running and hold his shirt like a basket.

Darrel stopped too close to the Sheriff and had to take a couple of steps back. "Here," he said. He dumped the contents of his shirt on to the ground. A dozen of the locusts fell at their feet. "See." Darrel handed one to the Sheriff.

"Grasshoppers?" He turned to Galvin. "You're wife gave us a couple of these back at your house."

Galvin didn't feel like talking. He moved further into the squad car.

The Sheriff turned to Darrel and handed him an evidence bag. "Put those in here."

Darrel filled the bag with locust. "They'd have eaten everything."

The Sheriff took the bag from Darrel and tossed it in the trunk with the evidence kit. "I think that I'm going to need you to come with me to the station. I'll have one of my deputies take your statement while I talk to Galvin."

On the ride to the station, no one in the car said a word. Darrel's earlier exuberance had quieted. Galvin was lost in thought about his son, his wife, his baby girl, and his farm. He didn't know how he was going to salvage any them. His could imagine his wife hating him for all of what transpired tonight. Somehow, it'd all end up his fault, and he hated that the most – that the loss of his son boiled down to his inaction.

As they turned onto the Highway and made their way east, the sheriff's radio squawked, "Ah, Sheriff, you there?"

"Go ahead."

"We've got reports coming in regarding a swarm of grasshoppers just south of your position."

Galvin shook his head, "They're not grasshoppers. They're *Melanoplus spretus*."

A Tea Party

Dan believed good things happen to people who give rather than take. Dan was young. He spent each morning helping his mother in the kitchen and around the house. He would notice that the dishes were dirty and do them without being asked. He'd see that the Sunday paper was spread around the living room, the comics on the ottoman, the sports pages on his father's lap, the jobs section here and there on the floor marked with red lines and circles. Dan would silently pick up and refold each section, making sure not to wake his father or disturb his mother. He'd reassemble it, setting it neatly on the coffee table.

Then at night, before bed, he'd take out the trash and move the cans to the curb in front of the house for Monday's pick-up. Dan would look for things that were out of place. He knew that if he could keep the little things from coming between his mother and father that they would love each other more, love him more. Good grades, Little League, keeping his bike in the garage where it belonged. Dan believed that it all helped.

One Sunday night, as Dan was making the rounds, picking up stray leaves, sticks, and pulling the occasional dandelion, he saw a shadow moving between the house and the garage. A shadow about his own size, shaped like a boy.

Being reckless, as young boys sometimes are, Dan didn't consider the danger that could have been waiting for a boy in the early night. He just went after the shadow, quietly sprinting, avoiding the dry leaves that would have crashed like thunder. A small girl in torn skirts stepped out in to the lamplight as he turned the corner to slide between the house and the garage.

She stood there, caught in the garage's floodlight where Dan would sometimes draw chalk pictures on the pavement. Her dirty blond hair was in two greasy pigtails. Her eyes were blue on top of purplish-black crescent-shaped bruises. The truly remarkable thing was her doll. It was one of those lifelike things with the big plastic head and the creepy eyes that opened and closed. It was pristine.

Dan didn't know what to do. He had thought in his boy's mind that one of the neighbor boys was goofing on him, and that he was going to engage in some kind of contest of stealth and speed; however, he was ill equipped to handle this: a dirty girl that looked like she belonged in the trash. Dan stood there looking at her. He was turning something around in his mind, something new, something that had never occurred to him before, but now seemed so simple.

He held out his hand to her.

She held her doll close, protectively. She turned to look over her shoulder as if taking some unspoken cue from the darkness. She then stepped forward and took his hand.

"My name is Alice." Pointing her chin at the doll, "This is Sally. She's my baby."

He felt her hand in his. Her hand was rough and cold. He thought that girls were supposed to be warm and soft. This simple touching of hands made Dan's face wrinkle and he began to wonder if he had done the right thing. But it was too late. She had told him her name and had put her hand in his. "I'm Dan."

"Hi Dan." Alice looked at her doll. "Say, 'Hi Dan,' Sally." Alice rocked her doll forward and it said, "Hi Dan," in a voice that didn't sound very much like Alice's.

Dan winced and let go of her hand. The doll had spoken. It must have been a recording. Some of the newer dolls could do that, he reasoned, even though it didn't seem very reasonable to him. Well, it was only polite that he answer back, "Hi Sally." He immediately felt foolish, his cheeks warmed.

Alice smiled a big dirty smile, showing many gaps where her baby teeth had fallen out. She put her finger in the gap in the front of her smile. "See. Papa told me that the boys like gap-girls. Do you like gap-girls, Dan?"

Dan knew something in what she had said was wrong. He squinted at her in the lamplight. "Where do you live?"

Alice looked him up and down. She looked over her shoulder. "Can you keep a secret, Dan?" She rocked her doll and Sally's eyes clicked shut then opened.

Dan felt as if Sally was going to say something, so he waited. He balanced on his toes then his heels, hands in his pockets.

"Dan?"

"Sure. Yeah." Dan moved a little closer to Alice as if this secret was to be whispered into his ear.

"In your backyard. The alley really. But your backyard. Me, Papa, Mama, my little brother, Sally, and all my other dollies."

Dan looked at Sally. The bright light danced on her plastic face. Her eyes were open. Suddenly, Dan felt in over his head. He wanted to do what was right. He wanted to help, but he was just Dan. His father wouldn't have liked that thought. His father was always telling him to be somebody. His father had told him that if someone was in need that he should help.

Dan's mouth felt dry. His tongue was thick with indecision. He had all the tools there in his mind. He was just about to take her hand again and make her come inside to talk with his parents, when Alice darted back into the shadows. Dan had made up his mind. He knew what to do. He ran after Alice. He had to help her.

Dan could see Alice near the fence that separated his yard and the alley. She was standing next to the gate. She was holding it open. In the crook of her left arm, Sally wore a desperate look. The light glinted off Sally's eyes. And for just a moment, Dan thought that he had seen a tear in one of Sally's eyes, wet and real. He stopped running, "Alice. Alice. Come inside with me. It's warm. We have food."

Dan thought that Alice looked stunned. She said something that he couldn't hear. He tried to see who she was talking to. He couldn't see anyone other than Sally. She must still be talking to Sally. She must.

Alice was standing next to him. Dan jumped.

"Dan." Alice took his hand. "Dan. Come with me. Meet my parents, meet everyone."

"No. Alice, come inside with me and have some hot chocolate. We have the kind with the little marshmallows." Dan squeezed her hand and turned to head back toward the house.

"No." She held on to his hand and planted her feet. She wouldn't budge. "Come with me."

Dan wasn't about to give up. Perhaps if he went with her she'd come around and return with him. She seemed to really want to show him something. Once she did, he'd ask again.

Dan was full of stories about adventures. His friends were always out getting into trouble. Over lunch, at school, they'd tell him of their adventures and how much trouble they were in with their parents. They'd go around the table, each telling a tale of some exploit that meant that they were grounded. When they'd get around to Dan, they'd laugh. Dan the man, they'd say, Dan the do-nothing man. Boring old Dan.

Dan had adventures, but they were not the kind of adventures that you share with your friends. They were the kind of adventures that get you punched and left for dead in the boy's bathroom with your shirt over your head and your pants around your knees. They were the kind of adventures that you kept to yourself.

Dan didn't like to talk about his adventures. They were his. Like the time his mother asked him to ride his bike two miles to the store and pick up fixings for salad: romaine lettuce, two tomatoes, carrots, olives, chives, and a bottle of dressing. Any dressing, she had said he could pick. Surprise me, his mother had said. She had trusted him with him a twenty dollar bill. That was an adventure. He didn't even know what romaine lettuce was. He had to ask, and asking was hard. But he got on alright and paid for everything on the list and made it home. Part of him had thought that he might not make it. That there was something out there, in the streets, that would try and stop him.

Dan wanted to have a real adventure, one that he could share around the lunchroom table with the other guys. With Alice leading him forward by the hand, it felt like one of those adventures that always happened to someone else. A smile crossed Dan's face. He was ready.

Alice giggled as they ran through the gate which led into the alley and the darkness that waited beyond the floodlight's reach.

Dan stood looking down at the dark hole in the pavement. Alice had slid the drainage cover off just enough that she could squeeze through. She had wrapped Sally in her skirts and climbed down. Dan couldn't wait for lunch on Monday. The guys wouldn't believe him.

They'd laugh. He knew they would, but he'd stick to his guns. He'd tell them that he went into the sewer with a girl. This was exactly the kind of adventure he had wanted. He'd only go down for a few minutes then he'd convince her to come back with him to the house.

Dan looked up to make sure that he knew where he was. He could see Jimmy's house and Jen's house and the stop sign that was bent over when the Murphy's oldest boy hit it with the truck. He wasn't very far from home at all.

"Dan," Alice called. "Hurry, Dan, before someone comes."

Dan climbed down into the dark. His shoe squished something at the bottom. It smelled foul. Like when his father forgot to flush. He couldn't see anything either, except lighter shades of complete darkness. "Alice." He held out his hands in front of himself and swung them side to side. "Alice, I can't see."

"Open your eyes, silly."

Dan took a deep breath and opened his eyes. He saw pink everywhere. Cotton-candy pink, everywhere, pink curtains hanging in front of a pink window. Pink cushions on a pink bed between pink dressers, pink everywhere. Alice's dress was perfectly pink. Dan looked around as if he had just entered the candy store on his birthday.

Alice was standing in front of a bookcase filled with dolls of all kinds. "Do you like my dollies?"

Dan took a closer look. One shelf had really fat dolls that were filled with smaller dolls. Another shelf had the kind he'd seen at his grandmother's, the kind with the wrinkled potato faces and beady black button eyes. One shelf had a row of baby dolls with bottles. He picked one up.

"Careful. Those wet themselves if you feed them."

Dan quickly put it back on the shelf. He turned to look at another row of small plastic ones. They had big heads and big eyes. When he picked up the one with brown hair and the firefighter's helmet, the head rocked back and forth as if it were on a spring. Dan could hear Alice giggle.

"Do you like my room?"

"You have a lot of dolls." Dan reached for a set of adult looking dolls. These were more like Barbie and Ken. These he knew. Jen had Barbies. These were dressed like Dan's parents would if they had to go to work. The Ken-like one even had a little briefcase in one hand and a newspaper in the other. The woman had a green purse and a cup of coffee. Dan picked her up. She looked a lot like an older version of Alice.

"Those are my parents." She picked up her father by his stiff plastic legs and held him out to Dan. "Here. You play Papa and I'll play Mama." She took the Barbie from him.

Dan took the one Alice held out for him. It was a doll. It was plastic. Its hair was molded perfectly. Dan held the doll so that he was looking at its profile. This doll had a belly that hung over its belt. Dan had never seen a doll that looked so life like before.

"Over here, Dan." Alice was pointing to a small doll-sized table on top of her dresser. "Set Papa there, please."

Dan folded the doll's legs so that it was in a sitting position and pushed it up to the table. "Okay."

Alice smiled. "Mama, say 'Does Papa want a cup of tea?'"

"Does Papa want a cup of tea?" the doll asked.

"Your turn Dan, tell Papa to say something back to Mama." Alice crossed her arms in front of her and waited.

Great, Dan thought, more talking dolls. He wondered how they worked. They seemed too small to have batteries. He picked his up and lifted the shirt in the back, looking for the switch.

"Dan! Put Papa down!" She stomped her foot. "Now!"

Dan snapped to attention. He looked at the little tea party. He closed his eyes and took a deep breath. He smelled flowers and mint. When he opened his eyes, Alice was still waiting for him. "Daddy, say 'Why, yes, I'd love some tea. Thank you.'"

Dan's doll spoke back the words he had given it. It wasn't his voice. It was deep and raspy. Before Dan could give this voice much thought, Alice's mommy doll picked up the tea pot and the daddy doll's tea cup. The mother doll poured the daddy doll a cup of tea, spilling just a little.

Dan watched as the two dolls enjoyed their tea. On the doll's table, next to the sugar bowl, there was a plate of cookies. "Daddy, say, 'Please pass the cookies.'"

The daddy doll repeated his words. The mommy doll passed the small plate. The daddy doll took one and ate it.

Dan thought the scene was nice. It was what he thought should happen between a mommy and a daddy. He looked at the dolls enjoying themselves. Dan didn't want it to stop. He looked around and felt like the other dolls were watching him, knew what he was feeling inside. He felt a tingling sensation wash over his skin. He shuddered.

Dan said, "Daddy, say, 'Thank you Mommy.'"

Alice looked at Dan. "Mama, say, 'You're welcome. Now, finish your tea.'"

As Dan heard the mommy doll say, 'you're welcome,' he pursed his lips. Something was wrong. It was just play, but it made him miss his parents. It was all too perfect.

Dan had had enough adventure. "Alice, I want to go home." And he moved away from her and the dolls. He turned to leave. He saw a door. He walked over to it. The door wouldn't open.

Alice touched Dan's shoulder while holding the mommy doll. "Mama, what do you think?" She waited.

Dan brushed Alice's hand off his shoulder. He tried the door again. "It's locked."

The mommy doll answered, "I like him."

Alice lay down on her bed and hugged a pillow to her chest. "You have to stay."

"No. I want to leave."

Alice waved her hand as if she were coming out from behind a curtain or finishing a curtsy. "They like you."

In unison, every doll stood and said, "Stay Dan. We like you."

Dan fell to the ground and pulled his knees to his chest.

"Oh. What's wrong Dan?" Alice asked.

"My parents..."

"They won't find you."

Dan screamed and banged on the door.

Alice set the pillow down. "How rude!"

"Help! I'm down here! Help me!" Dan kicked at the door. His eyes were clenched and wet.

"Stop it, Stop it. Stop it!" Alice gripped Dan by his hair and dragged him kicking and screaming towards her bed.

Dan whimpered.

Alice grinned through the greasy part in her hair. "You've been a very bad dolly."

Tagger

Signs

John Cougar cracked his knuckles by flexing and curling his fingers, each finger tattooed with a letter so that his fists spelled *weep-4-me-!*. He stood in a hot, dank alley between two Minneapolis warehouses off N Washington Ave and N 3rd Ave A breeze from the northeast, off the Mississippi River, kept the alleys cool. Cougar wore a white tank top and cutoff fatigues held up with rope. His arms were covered in dashes and dots that read, "The Truth is Out There," on his left and, "Trust No One," on his right in Morse code. He'd taken weeks to design it.

Cougar looked at his bike, tightened his messenger bag across his body, and took one last look at the writing. *Fuck*. He couldn't believe it. What writer would move into another's hood without paying proper respect? He'd have to deal with that later. He still had a few deliveries, and Big O didn't pay him to write. He got paid to peddle. Still, Cougar would have to deal with this joker soon. This was the third tag to crop up in his hood this week.

He slowly made his way through the streets past the newly Disneyfied Block-E disaster and the Target Center to swing north on S 8th St. His mind wasn't on the job. He kept moving, but he overshot the City Center and had to double back down Nicollet Mall, dodging suits and skirts on the sidewalks, not daring to compete with rush hour bus traffic. Cougar's mind was on the strange writing. He prided himself on being able to read any writing. It was just another code to be broken, but this had to be in some other language all together.

Cougar locked his bike to a No Parking Anytime sign and sat on the edge of a large concrete bowl, so-called functional modern art, filled with flowers, next to a guy tossing popcorn to a few aggressive pigeons. He unbuckled his bag and let it drop to his feet. He pulled out a pad of paper and a pencil. He sketched out the letters one by one, making sure not to overlap them as they were on the wall. He shook his head after finishing. He had to have been wrong. The words looked like nothing more than gibberish.

He put the paper away and picked up his bag. He had to get back in the game. He had a job to do. Cougar went into the City Center and up to the second floor where Target had expansion offices; the corporate campus on 11th St. S had been outgrown even before it had been finished. He didn't know what happened beyond the reception desk. He didn't know what he was delivering. He didn't really care. All he cared about was the time. His clipboard showed the time in and the time out, accompanied with signatures that he didn't bother to read. Keeping all that shit straight was Big O's job. Cougar's job was simply point A to B. His jobs this morning were important, but they weren't urgent. They were all nooners, as long he emptied his load before lunch, he was golden.

On his bike, Cougar made his way southeast toward the Convention Center's three red-brown domes. He cut through the alley between 8th and 9th, nearly spilling a violin case full of change. He barely noticed that the musician had stopped playing and was now yelling after him. Halfway through the alley he stopped and leaned his bike against a green dumpster. He walked around the side he'd just passed. On the end facing towards the angry musician, who'd started to play again, was a strange white symbol. This was even more disturbing than the writing had been. This one looked evil. The design looked familiar somehow: interlocking circles spiraling outward with a think line running though the center ending in yet another circle. He had trouble looking at it for more than a few seconds, after which his eyes blurred and tear up.

He felt the two tags were connected. It was a feeling he had deep in his gut. Yet, just as he knew they were connected, he knew they were written by two different writers. This was the first time he'd seen the pentagram, which meant that this writer was even newer than the last. He picked up his bike and rode through to Marquette Ave where he made another drop off, a long tube that most likely contained blueprints or some kind of art work. These tubes always interested

Cougar. He typically opened them and took a quick look-see. This one, like most, however, had been sealed. He wouldn't chance it.

As he left the building and unlocked his bike, green paint caught his attention. He rode across the street to The Foshay. The 9th St. side of the building had been tagged. The people walking up and down the street moved to avoid Cougar as he stood on the sidewalk straddling his bike. It was those letters again. This time they seemed to glow from within, as if they were windows looking out on to the street from some other distant realm, undulating with light and shadow.

For just a second, Cougar was able to take his eyes away from the vision. He looked to the people on the sidewalk. They walked as if with blinders, happy in their dark sunglasses and MP3 bubbles. Cougar couldn't believe that they'd just walk by and not notice. He wanted to pull grab someone and point it out. He wanted to ask someone if they could see what he was seeing. He picked a woman with a black handbag, pink heels, and white suit-skirt combo. But before he could grab her, his two-way squawked.

"Hot potato! Hot potato! IDS 10 to the River Monster."

That was Cougar's cue. Big O, the owner of Puddle Jumper Messaging and the messaging service's only dispatcher, needed him, nothing else mattered. Dan Ousts, Big O, was an ex-rider. He'd still be out on the street saddled into his custom single speed, but he had a disagreement with a sanitation truck and lost. He'd won a small sum of money from the lawsuit, but his lawyer jobbed him out of most of it. He'd been left with just enough to pay his medical and open his own service. Cougar didn't envy Big O. O's knee would never be the same.

"On it!" Cougar replied first. Carrying a hot potato meant money and cred if delivered on time. Cougar really didn't care about the added reputation. He just wanted the money.

Instead of locking his bike in the plaza, he slung it over his shoulder and ran in through the lobby to the security desk. He flashed his badge and ran for the doors that led to the elevator. He pushed his way into one that was about to close. He pressed the button for the 10th floor and called in.

"Toppings?" He ignored the murmurs and sour looks from the people behind him. The two men were holding Styrofoam containers that smelled liked stir-fry, sweet and greasy. It made his stomach growl.

"You got five to the Monster. A man in a blue pinstripe will be waiting by the 2nd St. entrance."

Cougar started to sweat. He'd have to push. This was going to be hard. By the time he reached the ground he'd only have a couple minutes left. He started rocking on his toes.

"Hey watch it."

Cougar had forgotten there were people in the elevator with him. He stopped rocking, "Sorry."

"I can't believe they let you in here with that thing."

Cougar watched the numbers, seven, eight. He started to mumble, "*Iä Iä...*"

"What'd you say?" The guy in the yellow tie and blue shirt kicked Cougar's back tire. "Piece of shit."

The elevator door opened. Cougar took a step forward and swung his tire knocking yellow tie's food out of his hands.

"What the fuck!"

The doors were already closing and Cougar was on his way to the floor's reception desk where a woman was waiting with a small envelope. Cougar handed her his clipboard. She signed and handed over the envelope.

Cougar caught an empty elevator on the way down. This time there was no one to stop his rocking and nervous bobbing. He was like a greyhound waiting for the rabbit and the gate to drop, tense and overexcited

When the elevator stopped and opened, he shot out and through the lobby and the front doors. Once on the street he saddled up and shot down Marquette Ave towards 2nd St. He didn't have time to think about creative shortcuts. He'd have to muscle through it.

"Cougar," squawked Big O, over the two-way, "ETA on that potato."

Cougar sat up on his bike as he dodged a bus. He pulled on the two-way, "Mashed."

"What? You got no time, bitch! Peddle!"

Cougar pony'd. Not watching where he was going, he almost ran down a woman crossing Washington Ave S with her walker. He knew she had yelled something but he was already a block away, turning down 2nd St S. His heart was pounding. He was never going to make it. He felt his mind drift as the edges of his vision blurred. He was riding harder than he ever had before. He hated being late for a drop. It looked bad for everyone, O, Puddle Jumpers, all messengers. He felt his body fighting back.

Without knowing why, breathlessly he started chanting those strange words he'd seen glowing on the side of The Foshay. His chat started out slowly, a mere mumble. As his mumblings turned into shouting, he started to froth at the mouth. White spittle bubbled up and ran down his chin.

In the middle of 2nd St. S., he saw a bright light that looked like the design he'd seen on the side of the dumpster. The circles rotated clockwise. He couldn't look away. He was going to ride straight through the spinning lights.

"Hey!" shouted a balding man leaning over Cougar in a blue pinstripe suit. "You have my tickets."

Cougar struggled to his feet. He slowly opened his bag, taking out his clipboard and the envelope. He felt more than just sick and exhausted. He felt as if something had reached down inside of him and scooped out a bit of his soul. He wasn't religious, but he felt less than whole.

"That was some spill." Pinstripe took his tickets, handed the clipboard back, and walked up to the entrance of The Guthrie Theater where a finely dressed woman waited.

Cougar looked at his watch. Somehow he had enough clarity to ask himself, who saw a play before noon on a Tuesday? Then again, he'd never been to a play that wasn't outdoors in a park or free.

Cougar sat down on the curb, letting his bike rest against a telephone pole. Using the two-way, "O, it's baked." Cougar waited. What the hell had happened? One minute he was riding like he never had before, the next he was... He couldn't put words to it. He shook his head.

"Fuck Yeah!" O shouted back. "That was a nasty run."

Cougar looked at his bag. He still had his nooners to finish. He felt limp and weak. Cougar called in, "O, I'm out. I need a snatch and grab at 1st Ave N and N Washington Ave."

"You earned it. Grab in 10. Take it easy."

Paint

Cougar sat on his black futon without his shirt clutching a beer that he had been nursing since he'd gotten home an hour ago. He looked down into the bottle and his stomach moved. He didn't understand why he felt so sick. He'd been on a boat before. He likened the way he felt now to how he had felt then. It was as if his body was trying to compensate for movement that wasn't really there, so that when he tried to walk he'd misstep, expecting the floor to rise up to meet his foot.

His mind kept racing back over that last run. He could clearly remember taking the corner at 2nd, but everything between that and handing the envelope over was a complete blur. He could swear that he'd looked at his watch and the time had been up. He'd failed, but somehow he'd made the delivery. It was as if time had not only stopped, but flowed backwards.

He put the beer down. He crossed the room to where he had dumped his bag and retrieved his notebook. He sat down on the floor. Cougar's apartment was bare except for the futon, a small TV on a milk crate, his bike, and a pile of spray paint cans. The walls were covered in colorful graffiti. He practiced his writing on the walls. Every couple of months he'd paint the walls white and start over. He had one small patch left open in the kitchen behind the refrigerator. He pulled it out of its place and pushed it in front of the countertop.

He shook a can of green, listening to the bead bang against the sides of the can. When he felt the paint was fully mixed, he let loose. His hands moved quickly with precision. He fell into the work. The loops and twists, it was like he was someone else. He had always felt like his writing let loose someone else contained within his skin. This time was no different. He let that other side of his self take over completely.

When he stepped back from it, he admired the shape of it. He thought that he had reproduced the mystery writer's work fairly well. It was that strange set of words that he kept hearing in this head. As he looked at them, they began to make sense. He ran his index finger through the wet lines on the wall.

Grabbing his notebook he wrote, We're here. Prepare for our coming. Cougar tossed the notebook against the wall. What the hell did that mean? He walked across the floor, put on his shirt, and grabbed his bike. He had to find the writer. He had to know what it meant. Who was coming, and why didn't they respect his turf, his canvas?

The strangest thing was that he had an idea of where to start looking for answers.

Crew

Cougar sat on the corner of one of the fountains in the Government Plaza watching the light rail as it headed for the Metrodome. It was empty. For some reason he knew that this was the next place that the writer would tag. He didn't know why he knew it, but he was positive. However, he'd been waiting for the better part of the day. It was starting to get cool as the sun went down behind the buildings. He wasn't going to budge. He was going to stay here all night if he had to. He wasn't going to move from this spot.

The red and orange marble tile that made up the plaza's walkways gave off an eerie light this time of day that Cougar had always liked. Tonight however, it wasn't comforting in the least. He found it repulsive.

There were a couple of guys with a video camera and skateboards near the steps and railings. They took turns filming as the other attempted some trick down the stairs, otherwise, the place was deserted. Cougar stood and walked to 5th St. and back to the fountain. He picked up a rock out of another large pot with white and purple flowers. He skipped it across the water in the fountain. It skipped twice before swerving out of the water to skid across the tile.

Cougar opened his bag and pulled out a can of green paint and started shaking it. He couldn't see anyone around. He looked at the open plaza and forgot why he was waiting, then he moved out into the center of the plaza between the fountain and the light rail stop. He sized up the area. He was going to put down one of his more ingenious designs, one that anyone would recognize as his, but as he started his mind began to slip. He had made a few lines when he heard a raspy female voice.

"I see you've started without me."

Without turning around, Cougar said, "Beat it."

"But that's my signature."

Cougar took a few steps back and looked at what he had been sketching. It was the eye of the pentagram from the dumpster. He bent down and touched the paint. He looked up at a slim figure in a hooded sweatshirt. "You're a she."

"Of course I am," she said. She pulled her hood down. Her hair was short and spiky. The tips were dyed orange. Her nose was pierced as was her lower lip. The left side of her face was covered in some tribal tattoo design. To Cougar it looked as if she had scales. "Are you going to tell me why you're copying me?"

Cougar looked back up at the design. "It's not what I...." If he had thought of it sooner, he would have placed fake tags around the city to draw her out. "I..."

"No need to explain." She held up her hand in a fist and then opened it and waved.

Several others appeared out of nowhere. One asked, "Is he ready?"

"Wrong color, but yes, he's ready."

"Then let's finish this, Sandra." One of the other women dropped her bag and rummaged through it. She pulled out a can of white paint and tossed it to the woman with spiked hair next to Cougar.

"J.C., right?"

"Cougar, I can't stand J.C." He backed out of the way.

"Cougar, okay. This is our last one tonight." Sandra and the others pulled out more cans of white paint. "How did you know to put it exactly here? Tonight?" The mixing beads sung like crickets.

"I just knew. I knew the way I know when and where traffic will be, how to dodge taxis and buses." Cougar was having trouble taking it all in. He had meant to sketch out his own tag. Instead, he had drawn the circles. The circles were creeping him out. They seemed to be suggesting direction and a target.

Sandra handed Cougar a can. "Come on, finish what you started." She squeezed his arm and went back to spraying with the others.

Cougar could hear the group beginning to chant, except their words were different. They weren't the horrible lines that haunted his sleep. He didn't know these words. He shook his can and stepped up. The others were swaying as they painted and chanted. Sandra was the only one with her hood down. Cougar thought that it might have been the fumes, but Sandra's face was blurring.

Sandra and the others, all women, began shedding their clothes. They stood naked in the center of the pentagram around the eye. Cougar forgot where he was for a moment, as he watched Sandra's body illuminated by the plaza floodlights. Then a strange red glow began to flicker. It made their flesh look orange. He could not take his eyes off them. Cougar could feel heat building up all around him.

Sandra walked over to him. "Let me." She gently helped him out of his clothes. "Watch, Cougar, and bear witness to the oldest struggle in the universe." She took his hand and led him into circles.

Cougar and Sandra joined the others. They joined hands with the others and held them up to an eye shaped moon. Cougar did not know the words, but he tired to join in with the chanting. Sandra's hand felt rough and dry in his hand. He tried to let go. Her grip was hurting him.

Then the chanting changed and Cougar knew these words. He couldn't resist them.

The streets filled with light from that seemed to originate from with in the circles. Cougar, barley conscious, couldn't believe what he saw. It was too much. He felt himself slipping, about to faint.

Sandra pulled his hands away from his eyes and held them up toward the moon. She pointed up. The moon looked like it was on fire; impossible red flames licked the surface.

Sandra yelled, "He's awake!"

"Look," another pointed.

Sandra kept her hands up. "May those who dwell in the infinite darkness protect us!"

Cougar could see something monstrous just above their heads. He didn't know how, but he understood that whatever it was; he knew it had come for him. He watched in terror as long serpentine appendages undulated out from the glowing sphere.

"Now! Do it now!" shouted Sandra.

Cougar couldn't explain where the knives had come from. Each of the naked women held what looked like daggers in their left hands. At Sandra's signal each of them plunged it deep into their chests. Cougar watched them fall towards the corners of the pentagram.

Cougar was left standing alone and naked. He looked at the bodies and moved to the center. He stood in a shower of light radiating down from the strangely shaped sphere. He felt as if he was on fire.

As Cougar succumbed to the fire, he saw the giant tentacles of retreat back into the sphere. His last thoughts were of the circles within circles in the sky as he slumped to the ground, and his mind into darkness.

The Man in the Mirror

Cougar woke in his apartment and started to thrash around and rolled onto the cold floor, where he rolled back and forth pulling the sheet tight. He was breathless, trying to hold on to what little air he had left in this lungs. As he flopped around like a fish out of water, he banged his head on a loose can of red paint. He called out, desperate and breathless. He sucked in air through his nose, then his mouth, dripping spittle.

Cougar stopped thrashing and opened his eyes. Through tears he looked around and realized that he was in his apartment. He unwrapped himself from the sheet and tossed it on the futon. He walked into the bathroom and ran water in the sink, splashing his face and rubbing the sleep from his eyes. He looked in mirror at his face and ran his fingers through his hair making sure that it was still there. He took a deep breath through his nose and swore that he could still smell the musky scent of burnt flesh and hair.

He got into the shower. He turned the water on hot. He felt completely covered in sweat and grime. As he stood in the shower letting it revive his weary body, he turned his back to the spigot. Hot water stung the skin on his back, making him jump away.

Cougar turned to face the water and took a step back. Thick red swirls of blood and black flakes pooled with the water as it ran down the drain. He twisted his head and felt his back. It felt as if he had stuck his hand into a bowl of oatmeal. He gritted his teeth as he brought his hand around. He saw bloody lumps of his skin drip from his fingers.

He pulled the shower curtain open leaving a bloody hand print. The mirror above the sink was fogged up. Cougar could only see his outline.

Running out into the hall he slipped and had to grab onto the door frame. He dripped into the living room and stood in front of a large wall mirror that had come with the place when he rented it. From the front he looked fine, except that blood was dripping down and around his legs to pool onto the floor.

Turning around and looking over his shoulder, Cougar saw an ugly mass of ripped and gnarled skin. He touched the base of his neck and his skin easily came off in clumps that sent pain shooting through his body. Sitting down on his futon he saw dark wet patches in the fabric.

He pushed his finger into one of the stains and it turned red.

Cougar spun around. He fell to the floor with a slick thud. He had tripped over a large squirt gun. He kicked it and ran from one side of the room to the other. He leaned there panting for a second, and then he ran to his window and looked out. He put his hand on the glass. He looked at the red smudge that he left there. He kept shaking his head from left to right and mumbling. In his nakedness, he started to shiver.

His two-way squawked. It was O, "Bitch, check out Fox."

The room was silent again. Cougar twitched. He flopped toward the TV. He found the remote. Shaking he dropped it. He left it on the floor and pressed the on button. His TV came to life. He reached over and pressed the up button twice.

A cop was saying something, Cougar couldn't make it out. The cop was standing next to an area sectioned off with yellow security tape. Behind the officer, on the tile, it looked like a pile of burned wood. The picture moved in for a close up on the officer's hand. He was holding a video camera and a couple of skateboards.

The camera swung back to the reporter, "If you have just tuned in, we are live in downtown Minneapolis, in the Government Plaza where a terrible crime occurred sometime last night. If you have any information about the three individuals in the following footage, please contact the police right away."

A very shaky picture came on. It was dark except for the Plaza lights, a kid on a skateboard executed a couple of tricks. He stopped and pointed behind the camera. He ran over, grabbed the camera and the other kid came into view for just a second as the picture focused in on a heavily tattooed nudist.

The nudist stood with his hands raised up to the sky. Then he looked in the direction of the camera. He picked up a giant super soaker and ran towards the camera. In the center of the nudist's chest there was a strange symbol that resembled the flaming eye that was in the center of all those strange pentagrams that Cougar had been seeing.

The nudist shot the camera and both of the boys. He then produced a lighter from nowhere. There was fire everywhere. The camera was dropped and the screen went black.

The reporter who came back on was saying something.

Cougar's two-way squawked, "What the fuck did you do?" Click, squawk, "If you're at home, get the hell out of there."

Cougar watched as the news replayed parts of the film again. He looked closely at the nudist with the strange circle tattoos. He looked down at his own chest and the same tattoos spun. Cougar gently touched the ink on his chest with his trembling fingers.

He walked over and picked up the gun. It was still heavy and smelled awful. He pulled the trigger and a long stream of gasoline hit the wall and splattered everywhere. Cougar dropped it to the floor and it broke open and more gas emptied onto the floor and over his feet.

Cougar slipped and fell. He lay there on his side, groaning. Without thinking, he rolled over on to his back. The gas stung worse than the water and he howled and thrashed. He stumbled over to his futon and tried to dry himself on a blanket. As he pulled the sheet off the futon, a lighter fell to the floor.

Cougar picked it up. He was shaking worse than ever now. He was hunched over and mumbling. He held the lighter in his hand and struck it. The flame jumped from the lighter to his hands to his legs to the floor. Fire was everywhere. Cougar just sat there mumbling as he slipped into unconsciousness.

The Man Who Ejaculated Ovum

One

Jake Duval was a man's man. His needs were simple. On the weekends, he'd rise before dawn, throw his two-person rowboat into the back of his Chevy F150, and make for his favorite smallmouth bass pond. He wore red-checkered 3M insolated flannel shirts, carpenter cut Lee blue jeans, and his construction grade steel-toed boots, none of which he'd purchased in the last five years. The only items Jake could bring himself to shop for were steaks and potatoes, parts and tools, and bait for fishing. After a long day of Saturday morning fishing, he'd drop down in front of the television to catch college football. It didn't matter who was playing. Sure, his favorite teams were Iowa State and the Nebraska Cornhuskers, but football was football. If any one thing were true about Jake Duval, it was that no one in his or her right mind would dare call him womanish. Well, except perhaps his childless wife.

Today was one of those Saturdays and Jake had just dropped down on the couch in front of the pregame show line up. His weekly Saturday morning fishing trip had been less then successful. Most of what he'd pulled in was underweight had to be thrown back. He loved to eat fish, but if he were to be honest, it was less about taste then having caught and killed the food on his plate. Still, he'd been lucky enough to pull two large ones into his boat. At least he'd provided dinner for tonight.

Sensing his wife enter the living room, Jake tied to calm his nerves. He knew what she wanted, and he knew giving it to her would cause him to miss the pregame show, which include upcoming games, recaps, and information about how the Huskers and Iowa State were progressing in the brackets. He loved her despite her timing. However, he loved football more than he cared to admit and would like to postpone fulfilling her needs until halftime. He felt halftime was designed to allow men a break in the action to feign interest in their wives, a design that he felt most women respected.

"Honey," she called in hushed tones that spoke of lace covered flesh, stain sheets, and sweat. "Why don't you get your pole and fish in my pond for awhile."

He knew that she wasn't asking, and he hated it when she used fishing metaphors to describe sex. He also knew that if he didn't answer her call, she'd switch up her game and start comparing sex with football. The last time she'd tried to seduce him using football, he hadn't been able to get the image of his favorite players passing him around in the locker room like some college bitch who'd bit off more than she could rightly swallow.

Well, there was no sense in keeping a fertile woman waiting. He'd hate it if she'd get around to gossiping with her friends anyway. He couldn't have rumors floating around that he'd turned his wife down. A man should be so lucky to have a fertile woman in heat, despite her bad timing.

He might as well play along, then. He stood up and turned around.

She was wearing black lace, which contrasted nicely with her pale skin and strawberry blonde hair. "Well," she said.

He made as if he were casting, and then he reeled back as if he'd hooked *the* big one. "I gots ya," he said. "Now, I'll reel ya in."

Two

Susan Duval sat with her husband in the fertility clinic waiting room. The room was painted an off white, perhaps eggshell. Everything lately reminded Susan of eggs, of sperm, of how things were supposed to work. She touched her empty abdomen. In the last three years, she'd read every book, magazine article, and website she could find on reproductive success. She'd even consulted a doctor and obtained a prescription that was guaranteed to increase contraception. At first she'd been afraid that she'd wind up like one of those women on TV with octuplets. That was a year ago. During that year she'd suffered what only she could call tumultuous periods. Periods with cramps that almost dislodged her sanity and flows that kept her home and in the bathtub, fearing that she'd frighten her coworkers. Because when her flow finally came, it was as if a dam deep with in her body had broken, it was nothing less than a tidal flood.

She looked at her husband. She loved him. She loved that he was willing to see her doctor. Her doctor had assured her that the problem didn't reside in her. With the medication she was taking, he'd never seen a fetus not take hold in the first three cycles, even when dealing with the least fertile couple.

"Jake," she said, putting her hand on his knee. "Thank you."

He put down the magazine. His eyes were deep brown pools of mystery behind lashes that could make a woman envious. "Sure," he said.

"You know what they're going to ask of you?"

"In a cup."

"In a cup." She smiled before kissing him on the cheek. His whiskers felt like a wire brush. "You going to need help?"

The smile on his face regressed his age so that he looked fifteen. "Do you think they'll let us," he looked around the office, "in there?"

"I don't see why not."

Susan looked away. She felt the heat rise in her cheeks under his boyish gaze. It felt good to know that he still desired her. She knew that she'd been pushing him hard lately with her schedules, timetables, and internal temperatures. She opened her purse and retrieved her pink lip-gloss. Suggestively, knowing that he was still watching her, she ran the gloss applicator over her parted lips. Putting the lip-gloss back into her purse, she uncrossed her legs and crossed them again so that she could lean into chest. Once there, she slipped her hand behind her back and down the front of his jeans.

"Susan." He picked up a magazine and held in between his knees.

She looked into his wide eyes. "Yes."

He looked around the office again. In the room, there were a few other couples, a few lone men, and a number of lone women. Not a one of them seemed to be giving them any mind. He squirmed then relaxed tipping his head back.

"Nothing, nothing," he said.

"That's what I thought." She didn't feel anything wrong with him. He seemed to be in working order, so what was wrong. Why wasn't he able to get her pregnant? It should have been simple: tab A in slot B.

The door next to the receptionist opened. A woman in white holding a clipboard held the door open. She called, "Mr. and Mrs. Susan Duval."

Three

Susan's doctor sat behind a large wooden desk. Jake thought the classic doctor's office a myth until today, but here he was with his wife in one of the most cliché doctor's offices he'd never had cause to imagine. On the wall behind the doctor's desk hung degrees and certificates. Jake couldn't make what they said, but he guessed they were there to help the weak looking man behind the desk feel superior. The walls were a sandy yellow akin to hotdog mustard. The chairs were brown plush leather that ensured that patients sat a head lower, submissive.

"So what was so important that we needed a sit down?"

Susan looked horrified. "Jake."

"That's alright, Susan." The doctor rubbed his baldhead with this right hand before removing his glasses. "Jake, if it wasn't serous, I wouldn't have called you in, you're correct." He set his glasses down.

"Out with it."

"Well, I really would like another sample to confirm the findings." He squinted. "I'd also like to run a body burden test. Do you know what a body burden test is?"

Jake turned to Susan. "He's talking circles. Do you understand what he wants?"

Susan took Jake's hand in hers. She turned to look at the doctor. "We're simple people. Can you tell us your suspicions? What are you looking for?"

The doctor held up a pamphlet and handed it over to Susan.

"Atrazine," she said reading the cover. "What is Atrazine?"

"I hope that the reading material will explain what I'm unable to convey to you today or point you to reliable resources." The doctor took a sip from his coffee mug, which read: #1 DAD.

Jake had about had enough of this doctor, but he could see that Susan was about to tear up. He didn't want to add to her stress, so he took a deep breath. "Can you be straight with us? What does Atrazine have to do with me, our baby making?"

"Well, like I said. I'd like to obtain another sample and draw some blood for the body burden test to be sure." The doctor smiled. "Tell me, Jake, how have you been feeling lately? Any, uh, sudden physiological changes, such as weight gain, bloating, tenderness of skin, or hair loss?"

Jake, without thinking about what he was doing held his right hand over his left pectoral muscle. "No, I don't think so."

"Okay. If you do experience any such symptoms or any strange symptoms or sensations, I would like you to contact me right away." The doctor handed over his card. "And please, call me Radish."

"Okay, Radish, worst case scenario?"

"Good. Being familiar is good, don't you think?"

Susan screamed.

Both the doctor and Jake looked at her.

Calmly, she said, "Please tell me what is wrong with my husband."

"Susan, I was just about to get to my suspicions, but what I need you to understand is that they are only suspicions until I can get the results back from the body burden test and the a new sample from Jake, here. However, I can see that you won't allow me to double check the findings before revealing my theory."

Jake took both of Susan's hand his. "We're ready."

Four

It was Saturday again, and Jake was out on water. He'd cast his line and was slowly jerking and reeling it back. He had to catch a male. He had to understand why the doctor was so excited over his diet of fish, especially smallmouth bass. Sure, in the few days after he gotten the news – infertile – inconclusive – ovum mixed with semen – he'd searched out any and all articles concerning Atrazine.

The best of which were published by the New York Times and archived online. The New York Times had even put together interactive maps of the country showing lake and stream contamination levels. He'd zoomed in on his neck of the woods, his favorite fishing spots, and he was shocked to see that the levels were considered dangerously high.

The US Fish and Wildlife Service had even reported finding male smallmouth bass in various stages of sexual transformation. One example discussed had all the male parts necessary for reproduction, but it was producing only female ovum – effectively sterile. The report went on to say that Atrazine levels, if connected to the strange sexual transformation, would account for the significant drop in fish populations.

As Jake cast his line again, he sniffled and sobbed like woman. "Damn it." He let the lure sink into the water. He'd cast it into clear water away from the flowering lily Pads. He focused on his technique. He focused on fishing. He had to catch proof. He needed to see it for himself.

He just couldn't believe that an herbicide approved for use by the US Department of Agriculture could be so toxic as to alter the sex of fish. It was also shocking to learn that the United States was the only country practicing industrial agriculture in which Atrazine was approved for use. It had been banned in almost every other industrialized country, including many of the counties that produced it. Despite those bans, Atrazine was still included as an ingredient in many other herbicide concoctions.

While mulling over what the doctor had told him about how animals higher on the food chain were more likely to concentrate toxins, he left a tug on his line. Jake snapped back on the line, setting the hook. Whatever he had on the line – he hoped it was a smallmouth bass and not a catfish – it took off under the boat.

He let out the line. The fish needed to swim, and he was going to let it swim a little so that his line wouldn't snap. Getting into position, he set his feet under the forward bench. Then he stopped letting out line and the fishing pole bent drastically. Whatever he'd caught it was big. At least he'd hoped it was big.

He started to reel the fish in. The line was tight, so he reeled slowly. Perhaps, he'd get lucky and the fish would swim back towards the boat. He wasn't going to hold his breath for a lucky moment. He'd never seen a fish double back yet, and he was sure that the trend wasn't going to change today. Why should he get lucky? It seemed that his luck was to become some kind of laboratory freak — a man who produced ovum instead of ova.

It was no wonder that Susan was upset. She'd spent the last three years of her life feeling inadequate. If Susan was anything like Jake, she also feel a deep sense of relief at knowing that the enemy wasn't her body. At least he hoped that she felt some relief, but they had only gotten the news a few days ago, and it hadn't quite sunk in that they'd never be able to have a child of their own.

The fish was close. Jake grabbed the net in his left hand, still holding the pole in his right. He reached over the side of the boat and scooped up the fish. He brought it into the boat. It was a smallmouth bass and it was male.

Quickly, he took a hammer to bass's head. It stopped struggling against the hook and for oxygen. Jake found his fillet knife and cut into the bass. He'd usually make careful fillets, avoiding bones and internal organs, but this time he went for the belly toward the tail. When he cut into the male's sex organs, a thick black puss oozed onto his knife. He fingered the stuff, which smelled rich like wet earth. Between his fingers, the round jelly-like eggs burst and popped.

Jake, in his flannel, jeans, and boots, wept openly.

Five

Susan looked at Jake. He was in the yard, shirtless, with Nate, their German Sheppard. She didn't recognize the Jake she'd fallen in love with years ago. His well-defined muscles were softening. His Adam's apple disappeared. His pecs, one of his nicest features, were beginning to droop. He'd even lactated this week, wetting the front of his work shirt in front of the guys on the job with him. Worst of all was that his voice had raised an octave. She couldn't take his transformation any longer. She wasn't a strong woman.

Today was most likely Susan's worst moment. She couldn't watch her husband turning into...she didn't know what. She pulled an index card out of the junk drawer in the kitchen. She wrote down an address and the word: SORRY. She placed her wedding band on the index card.

She looked out the window once more. She'd thought that she'd feel more anxiety about leaving Jake to whatever fate awaited him, but she couldn't bring herself to feel anything.

On her way out the front door, suitcases in tow, her thoughts turned to fish. She'd never eat another fish again in her life. She hated the earthy smell, the fishy smell. No matter how it was cooked, she hated fish. Now, she'd never have to fry, poach, or bread another fish again.

Selfishly, perhaps to protect her feelings, she believed that he deserved it. He deserved to be changed forever by the one thing he loved more than her. She just wished that she could understand what the doctor's findings really meant. How it was that her husband was becoming feminized, chemically transformed from the man she had loved into something not manly and not womanly either, something in between.

The doctor had said that the smallmouth bass ate algae and insects that ate plants that were exposed to high levels of the weed killer Atrazine. The Atrazine had concentrated – or something – in the flesh of the fish, and just like DTD had affected the fertility of birds that ate DTD resistant insects, the fish and her husband's fertility had been impacted by over exposure to the weed killer.

As she closed the door on the freak show that was her husband, she felt a sense of finality and relief. She was free. She put her hand on her abdomen. It wasn't too late for her. She'd find another man, a man with sperm for her eggs. She was determined to have a child. After loading her luggage into the back of her car, she thought about

Jordan. Jordan had been eyeing her at the gym. Yes, Jordan. She'd start with Jordan.

She pulled out into the street. She knew that Jake would be a wreck when he found her ring on the kitchen counter. His nerves – no his emotions – were out of control. He was more womanly than she was, now. He was the drama queen. Well, the labs could have him and his drama, his strange ovum ejaculate. She suddenly saw herself as a fish that'd escaped the net by breaking the line. She would be the one who got away. She wished him the best. Then she never thought about him again.

Aaron M. Wilson

The Birthday Party

Moscow, August 10, 1961

Oleg Vladimirovich Penkovsky wet his comb with hot water that streamed from a polished silver tap. Music played downstairs. He raked his thinning red hair back into place. Parties could never move quickly enough for Penkovsky. First there were the arrival announcements. Then when the last name on the list was crossed off and sounded, a period of casual conversation ensued lubricated with Vodka and caviar. Even if this stage of a party was Penkovsky's favorite, for all the gossip that was spilt, it was always followed by a speech, dinner, more socializing, another speech, even more socializing, and finally departures. He finished combing his hair. He dried his comb and slipped it into the back pocket of his Russian colonel issue dress slacks. To think, all this was for a birthday party. Penkovsky thought he had better things too do than attend birthday parties. Russia had better things to be about than birthdays. He pulled his uniform's coat closed buttoning the large brass clasps. He double checked his State Committee for Science and Technology ID badge. Unfortunately for Penkovsky, useful and interesting things were often accidentally divulged at birthday parties.

The music was getting louder. Penkovsky could not stay hidden away in the General's lavatory forever. He had made his entrance earlier with General Ivan Serov the head of the Soviet Military Intelligence. Penkovsky had said, "If I'd known that being an intelligence officer would require me to attend all these parties..."

"You'd what?" asked Serov.

"I'd have rethought your invitation."

"My invitations are not really invitations. Besides, parties are very useful. Vodka and friends are the best truth serum."

"But here? Are we spying on our own countrymen?"

"Spy, bah, is such a western word. We safeguard. But, yes, we, you and I, must only think of what is best for the Soviet Union and ultimately Mother Russia."

"So what are you saying?"

"I'm saying that even I could, one day, unknowingly betray Russia, and that is why we exist and why we attend parties. You must learn to love cake, Oleg."

Penkovsky did not hate cake, but he did not care for it either. Penkovsky loved women. Women were the real Russian delicacy. If there was a redeeming quality to parties, it was the women. At fifty-two, Penkovsky thought he had finally mastered the art of seducing women. Tonight he wanted Lena, the daughter of Soviet Premier Nikita Khrushchev. She was dressed in a white lace gown with her black hair piled and pined atop her head showing her long neck strong cheekbones.

"If you go down that road, even I will not be able to save you," said Serov. "Have some more Vodka."

"Thank you," Penkovsky took bottle and a glass. "Look at the way she holds herself. She is majestic."

"She is dangerous."

Penkovsky took a drink feeling the slick heavy oil caress his tongue before sliding down his throat. Servers emerged carrying trays of lamb and stewed tomatoes. They placed a plate and a small bowl in front of each guest, like dominoes conversations stopped and guest took their seats. When the last server exited and the door swung closed everyone stood and faced the head table.

Serov whispered, "I think you will like this."

Penkovsky watched as Lena straightened her dress over her trim body. He might hate parties, but he loved party dresses. The way they showed off a woman's shape, the way they fluttered as woman clicked by in her heals.

Premier Khrushchev stood last. "Today we are here to honor the sixty-second birthday of my good friend, Sergei Varentsov." Premier Khrushchev turned to his left holding his wine glass high. "To Sergei, may he see many victories!"

The gathered guests cheered, "Victory," and sat down.

"Thanks to the Chief Marshall's missile program," Premier Khrushchev continued pacing his hand on Varentsov's shoulder, "It is time to strike a crippling blow to The West…"

Serov leaned back. "Now if you were really good, you'd already know what is coming, Oleg."

Penkovsky stopped ogling Lena. This was another reason why he hated parties, important people making important announcements while the food got cold. He felt less than Russian preferring his food hot.

"…We're going to close Berlin…"

Penkovsky chocked.

"…We'll just put up serpentine barbed wire and the West will just stand there like dumb sheep; and while they're standing there, we'll finish a wall." Premier Khrushchev held one hand in the air and made a fist. "For Russia!"

Premier Khrushchev waved the room down. "You are the first to know." He moved back behind his seat. "You are they only ones to know. Trucks, loaded with men and wire, are already on the move. We will show The West. We are strong!" He took his seat. "Now, eat, be merry."

In true Russian style, the gathered sat without another word and began eating.

Penkovsky had forgotten about Lena. He opened his uniform's coat and pulled out a small red monthly planner. He flipped to the back page labeled "Birthdays." He scanned the down the page by Chief

Marshall Sergei Varentsov's, the next birthday listed was Jean, September 10th. He closed the planner and his eyes. Jean Suiet and many of the bogus names listed on the birthday page were really code for his scheduled international technology gathering trips where he'd debrief his real employers, the American CIA. Jean meant that his next trip would be Paris.

Serov smiled. "Oleg, Oleg. You are not a good Russian. Leave business for later. Eat. Enjoy the Party."

Penkovsky pursed his lips and picked up his fork and knife. "You are right." He cut into his food. "You. You should have told me, you know."

"I need to have some surprises." He took his wine glass and smelled the wood and spice bouquet. "Keeping you on your toes is not easy, Oleg. Tonight gave me pleasure, knowing that I can still keep some secrets a secret."

"You know Ivan. I might learn to like these parties."

The Sirens of the Chipped Plate

(or, what happened after the club)

After the froggy demise of the self-professed fairy princess, a vacuum in the power dynamic of the girlfriend-entourage threatened to smudge perfectly glossed lips and stain foundation-fresh pallets and rosy cheeks with dark rivers of supposedly tear-fast mascara. Without the astute guidance of the self-professed fairy princess, the girlfriend-entourage sought comfort in their post-club routine and rendezvoused at Chipped Plate, taking up their reserved cracked yellow vinyl booth. Even though they could have brightened any table in the city, and likely been comped their meal with a simple batting of lashes and a few well timed giggles, they preferred to slum it up at CP's after a high-octane night of raving. The comfort afforded them through routine, provided the needed dash of normalcy for the girlfriend-entourage to reflect on their new freedoms. Thus, they each began to scheme, one of them needed elevation, and they needed a recruit, because everyone knows an entourage of two or three is not an entourage but a group of friends and four is an unlucky number.

While the girlfriend-entourage touched up their lips, re-applied their mascara, and teased out their glittered dusted hair, a lottery was underway just on the other side of the kitchen doors. The lead server produced the deck of cards used to pass the time until the clubs closed, forcing such royalty as the girlfriend-entourage to seek sustenance. After a quick shuffle, which would have impressed even the most veteran card shark, she fanned them out for her staff to draw.

"Low card wins *their* table."

They each took a card. Many of the servers held their breaths and their cards against their white shirts and blouses.

"Okay. Show'em."

Rex held up the Two of Spades. He pushed greasy strands of paper bag brown hair off his sunburned and flakey skinned face. Suddenly, his bloodshot eyes rolled into the back their sockets and his legs became overcooked asparagus limp as he collapsed. Now, the lottery and Rex's fainting spell would have all but gone unnoticed by the girlfriend entourage, but Rex had the added ill-luck of fainting into the service doors, which swung wide, spilling Rex into the dinning room. As soon as Rex hit the floor, he rubber-balled back up, onto his feet; and with out missing a step, he lurched over to the booth furthest from the safety of the kitchen, under the painting of the Spoon who jumped over the Moon, occupied by the girlfriend entourage.

"Coffee? Juice? Something to start?"

Compacts snapped closed. Where frowns had begun to creep, smiles appeared like Spring's first tulips. A man had spoken, and despite that man being Rex of the Chipped Plate, without the self-professed fairy princess out sparkling the others, the girlfriend-entourage competed for his attention. In a mad dash of adjustments, each of the four girls hiked hemlines shorter, pushed breasts up higher, sat up straighter – shoulders back, and legs crossed at their ankles.

Rex did not even try to contain his eyes. They roved over each of the girls, taking in every flirtatious gesture. They had him. He was theirs now. Enchanted so completely that when one of the girls finally ordered, he had to force his mouth closed and wipe a bit of drool from the corner of his goofy smile.

"Um, I'd like...um," with a flip of her hair, "a chocolate cherry cola and an order of those...um, shredded potato patty thingies."

"Ooo!" squealed the rest of the girlfriend entourage, "Us too."

Unaware that one of the girls had just scored a minor victory over the others, Rex tried to escape to place their table's order. He was barely able to tear his attention away. He turned body first, feet then hips and shoulders, followed by the painful whiplash of his neck. Once fully facing the kitchen, the spell that the girlfriend-entourage had cast upon him diminished with each step and fully dissipated as he slid beyond the service doors. In the kitchen, he was greeted by the rest of service staff, the busers and dishwashers, and the cooks.

"They," he stammered, "four chocolate cherry colas and four side-orders of hash browns."

One of the cooks piped up, "…chocolate cherry colas? We don't…"

"…but you will," completed Rex.

While the overnight crew of the Chipped Plate discussed pairing of chocolate cherry cola and hash browns, plots were being hatched by the girlfriend entourage.

"What was that, Melody? I don't even like cola," said Tiffany. "And like…what are shredded potato patty thingies anyway?"

"Yeah," added Tawny, "how dare you order for us."

Becky piped up, "I like chocolate cherry cola and hash browns."

"Shut up, Becky," Melody, Tiffany, and Tawny said collectively causing a jinx moment of pinky tugging.

"But…,"Becky said, "We need a leader. I feel lost, and I think that Melody fits the bill. She's pretty. She has good fashion sense. And did you see what she did to the waiter?" She paused for effect, unbelieving that she'd been allowed to say so many words in a row before declaring, "I vote for Melody."

"Vote?" Tawny stood wobbling a little on her stiletto healed pumps, "Vote? This is not a democracy. "We," she pointed her acrylic nails around the table, "are not a democracy!"

Cowering, Becky asked, "How then will we choose?"

"We don't," said Tiffany, "*choose*."

"Then, *How*?" asked Becky.

"In order to be the next princess, one of us must lure a worthy prince to acknowledge our worth by the lavishing-on of gifts to win our hearts..." started Melody.

Tiffany continued, "...before breaking his heart..."

"...and she must recruit our fifth," finished Tawny.

"That will take too long," complained Becky. "We have obligations, parties that we must visit, lest we get replaced. Besides, *we*," she pointed 'round the table, "don't need a man to decided for us."

Unfortunately, Rex picked that exact moment to set his serving tray beside the booth. He had kept his eyes on his shoe laces and his mind on his shoe's desperate need of a shine in the hope that he'd stay free of the girls' spell. Without knowing it, they had done him a favor by ordering the exact same dish and drink. He need not look up at any of them. He need simply place each glass and plate before escaping back into the kitchen. However, when he heard Becky defiantly proclaim their need for a man, he slipped and looked up.

"What's this? You don't need a...," Rex stopped mid thought.

Becky took the opening to re-affirm her position, "See. They are weak. They are slaves to our enchantments. We don't need them. I vote..."

"...*which* is why we need a prince," said Tawny. "They're immune."

"But Becky is right. We don't have time. We have obligations," said Tiffany. "We need to decide tonight. I propose we use this guy," pointing at Rex. "I say that we dawn the livery of the Chipped Plate, and see who he chooses."

"No make up."

"...or glitter."

"The one of us whose beauty needs not shimmer shall be the new princess."

In a moment of showy brilliance that threatened to stop traffic out side the Chipped Plate, the girlfriend-entourage stood and leaned over the table to high-five, a move that almost caused four simultaneous wardrobe malfunctions. After sitting back down and taking a drink from their chocolate cherry colas, they released their hold on Rex, so they could discus their proposition with him.

Melody took lead, "You will judge us."

"What?" asked Rex.

"Yes," said Tawny, "judge us."

Becky added, "We need you to help us decide which one of use should lead the pack, be princess while the others attend."

"I already have a jog," said Rex. "I don't like it, but who does? It pays the bills."

"Bills," asked Tiffany. "What are *bills*?"

"Oh! I know," said Melody. "I give those to Daddy."

Rex took two steps back. He was about to run back to kitchen when the girlfriend-entourage noticed his retreat. They stood again. This time, they surround him as Nymphs would their Satyr. Circling, they whispered into his ears.

Pick me. Pick me. I'm the one. What do you want – I'll see to it, just pick me. I'm prettier. I'm prettier. I'M PRETTIER.

As suddenly as they attacked Rex, they stopped. They stood between him and the kitchen, a wall of legs, glitter, and lip-gloss. They each removed a feather-extension from their hair and clipped it to Rex's black apron: Red, for Tawny; Pink, for Tiffany; Green, for Becky.

"Who every you pick, give her this." Melody handed Rex a blue feather hair extension. "She will know what to do."

They spun on the balls of their toes, as their heals would have stuck in the carpet and caused them to fall, and catwalk stomped into the kitchen. Leaving Rex in the empty dinning area of the Chipped Plate to ponder what had just occurred. He remotely recognized that he had been asked to judge the beauty of the four girls who had ordered chocolate cherry colas and hash browns. He had to pick one over the others when, to Rex, they were all of equal beauty. Sure, they one had green eyes, another brown, and yet another blue. One had blond hair; one had red, while the other two had chestnut brown. One had...he could go on and on, but each of them enchanted his very core. Thus, a thought happened across his frontal lobe, a solution to everyone's trouble, including an itch that he needed starching.

Sure. He felt dirty for even thinking about the proposition, but he felt that he didn't have anything to loose by asking them. They'd all likely shrug his request off like a dog biting a flee. He walked over to where he could see himself in the security mirror hanging in the corner, not far from the girl's booth. He didn't much care for what he saw there, but he said the words anyway. "Mirror, mirror, on the wall, will I score tonight."

"Ha!" The face in the mirror said. "Look at you, just talk a good look."

Rex Looked.

"See," the mirror continued, "your muscles are small. No doubt your idea of a workout is a five-hour First-Person-Shooter fest. Oh! Oh! And don't get me started on your complexion. Do you even wash that greasy mug of yours, or your hair?"

The kitchen door squeaked open. Rex turned around.

"Listen," coached the mirror, "you can't help them, but I can. If have them stand before me, I will whisper to you. However, there is a price..."

Rex thought his conversation with the mirror hadn't helped. He was still suck with four beautiful girls who wanted nothing from him other than his assessment of their beauty. They were all gorgeous, even as the walked over in the Black & White uniforms of Chipped Plate servers. Strangely, now that girls had removed their makeup, glitter, and straightened their hair, they were even lovelier. Uniforms. What was it about uniforms that Rex liked?

Tiffany stepped forward. "What do you think?" She spun on the toe of the black non-slip shoe as if she were a Swan in *Swan Lake*, a perfect pirouette.

"Stop that," said Tawny. To Rex she said, "Well, which one of us is prettier?"

Rex sat at the table that was to his right. The table would only sit two. "You are all wonderful. I think even more so than when you were made up."

"See. See, I told you." Melody pointed at Rex. "He's just a boy. He can't help us."

Rex looked into the security mirror to reassure himself that he was still in the room. He was. However, he noticed that he couldn't see three of the girls. The only girl whose reflection he saw was Melody. Rex shook his head. He was sure that Melody would lead this gaggle well, but they were asking for his input, and he didn't know when, if ever, his input would be needed again. So, he was going to make the most of it.

Rex said, "Look. I would like to speak to each of you individually." He pointed to the chair across the table from where he sat. "If that would be okay that is?"

The girlfriend-entourage huddled for a second before Melody stepped forward and stood beside the table. The others went back to their booth.

Melody continued to stand. After an uncomfortable few seconds, she coughed and tilted her head at the chair.

"Yes," said Rex, "please sit."

Melody coughed again, and she titled her head at the chair and smiled an awkward smile.

"Oh!" Rex stood, walked around the table, and helped Melody into the chair.

"Thank you."

Rex's interviews went well. He was surprised just how badly each of the girls wanted to be princess. They had each promised to fulfill his wishes in the most creative way. Well, all of them had agreed and more, except for Becky.

"You want what?" asked Becky.

Rex countered, "I think that you heard my proposition clearly. Look at me." He paused for effect. "When will I have such an opportunity," he winked, "again."

"No."

"No?"

Becky put her clutch on the table. It was covered with green sequins that threw of rainbows at odd angles. She pushed back from the table so she could cross her legs. She took out a lipstick the same shade of green as her clutch. She slowly turned her lips from her natural pale pink to a dark crabapple green. She flipped her hair over her shoulder before standing. She pushed her chair back into the table and leaned over it as if she were going to kiss Rex on the lips.

"Some times," Becky whispered, "the price is too high."

Rex had watched her walk over to the both where the others sat and giggled. He snuck a look into the security mirror. He could still only see Melody's reflection. It was as if none of the other girls existed to the mirror, only Melody.

Rex placed the blue feather hair extension on the table and stared it so intently that the wrinkles that creased his forehead threatened to pop several angry blemishes. He'd decided, against his better judgment, but he'd decided. Thus, he picked up blue feather hair extension and walked over to the girlfriend entourage's booth, where they were still nursing their chocolate cherry colas.

The girls, except for Becky, attempted to get Rex's attention one last time by batting their eyes, flipping their hair, and crossing and uncrossing their legs shifting suggestively, to which he seemed oblivious.

Rex seemed to deflate. He'd had his fun. Even if the girls would fulfill their promises to him, which he thought they'd rig on latter anyway, he wouldn't have been able to seal the deal anyway. He just wasn't that kind of guy. He'd always thought himself to be a player, but now, when the game was staring him in the face and eager, he felt only disgust at his behavior.

He lifted his eyes and looked deeply into each of their eyes, stopping and lingering on Melody. The mirror was right. Melody was naturally more beautiful. She glowed. Perhaps, she was part fairy. As these thoughts passed through his Rex's mind, Melody's skin began to shimmer, and he pictured the way her lips would look and feel as she fulfilled his fantasy. It should be her. Her promise had been the most intriguing and innovative, and the mirror confirmed it.

Rex took another step toward their booth. The excitement around the booth was contagious. Other guests, yes, the Chipped Plate had started to fill up with the hungry after-hours crowd, turned around just in time to see Rex hand the blue feather hair extension to Becky.

Stunned, Becky held it at arms length as if the hair extension might bite her. Strangely, as Becky held the blue feather hair extension, the feather came alive in her hand. The feather wiped back and forth in her had as if it were truly a snake. From somewhere in the Chipped Plate, someone screamed as the blue feather hair extension jumped from Becky's hand into her hair.

Once in her hair, as if a fairy godmother had waved her wand, Becky was lifted from the both into the air. The Chipped Plate attire transformed into a sleeveless blue dress that sparked with a plunging neckline, with no back to speak of, and with a mid-thigh hemline. The non-slip black shoes were replaced with heels. Her green clutch turned blue. Finally, her hair and makeup were suddenly salon fresh.

When whatever had lifted Becky from the booth set her down on her feet next to Rex, a rainbow cloud of glitter shot out in all directions. Everyone in the Chipped Plate was cheering and on his or her feet. The scene was grotesquely magical.

"Why me?" Becky asked Rex.

The other girls, now completely under the charm of the newly appointed self-professed fairy princess, clearly also wanted to know but could not ask. They got up from the booth and dutifully formed up behind Becky.

"You said, 'No.' And I respect that."

Becky nodded. She turned to *her* girlfriend-entourage and said, "You all agreed to..." She stopped. She couldn't say it. Then she turned back to Rex. "If it is in my power to grant you one," she paused, "reasonable request fro your help tonight, I will. Just name it."

"Start leaving tips." Rex said. "We work hard here, and you stiff us every time you come in."

"Is that all?"

"Yup, I guess so."

"Done."

When the girlfriend-entourage had reclaimed their magic, they left, but only after leaving tip. With Becky at point, they made a spectacular exit from the Chipped Plate. As if by magic, their limo pulled up to the curb. Then they were on their way again, everything was almost all right with the world. They were still short one girl. They needed someone to take up the mantle of the green feather hair extension.

Tiffany spoke up, "How do we find a fifth on such short notice?"

In her new position, Becky said, "Well, I think that's a story for tomorrow. Look at the time. We need our beauty sleep." To the driver, she said, "Take us home please."

"Kicking" Eve

Adam's brow creased and his right hand rose to his mouth, deeply in thought. "Grass," he spouted, "Grass." Then he performed a touchdown-like happy-dance before running over to Eve.

"Eve. Eve, guess what we're walking on. Come on guess."

Eve would look down at her bare feet, which she'd just learned not to long ago to be "feet," and that feet are to be used for "walking," "running," and "stomping" on little black things that Adam called "bugs." She shrugged her shoulders knowing that Adam would hate her for not trying.

"Come one, try to guess." He hated Eve's resistance to what he called the "Game of Naming." She was interested for a little while, a full cycle of the moon to be exact, so Adam had called that period of time "Month." Eve had been interested in his game for only a month, and he hated her for it, but he didn't have a name for the feeling he was having towards Eve. He'd have to get to that later. "Please, try."

Eve just shrugged her shoulders again and looked at Adam with droopy despondent eyes. "Just tell me so that I can know."

Adam kicked Eve in the side with one of his feet. "That is called, 'kicking,'" he said, having a moment of brilliance. Adam quickly kicked her again.

"Stop." Eve pulled away. "I don't like this 'kicking.'"

Adam was not used to Eve disliking any of his named things. He felt his face tense up and wrinkle along his nose, above his eyes, and around his mouth. Adam thought, this is 'frowning.' Then, because he didn't really like the way 'frowning' felt, he told Eve that the small green strands poking up from the ground, tickling and cushioning their every step was called 'grass.' Then he wandered off in search of new things to name.

Well, as you can imagine, Eve was bored with Adam's "Game of Naming." She wondered why she always had to be the one to guess and Adam the one to name. Then, after many of Adam's 'months,' Eve came across a tree with large red things hanging from its branches. Eve thought aloud, "I bet Adam has a name for this type of tree and those red things already."

"No, he doesn't," hissed the tree. "I bet you could name both the type of tree and the red fruit that hangs in it." A long body appeared out from between the leaves with a flat head and beady eyes.

Talking things were not new to Eve. It seemed that may things could talk, but very few of them ever had anything good to say. She questioned this thing. "And what has Adam called you?"

"Oh, Adam has not given me a name. I have named myself. I am a 'snake.'" The snake dropped out of the tree and landed in the grass next to Eve.

Eve puzzled over this 'snake.' "How can you name yourself?"

"Because I know myself."

"How?"

The snake looked up into the tree. It snapped its tail around one of the red fruits and pulled it free from the tree. The snake handed it to Eve. "I didn't know myself from the grass you walk on. Then I ate one of these, and I too had the power of Adam, to know and name."

Eve looked at the snake and thought about Adam and the "Game of Naming." With determination, she bit into the fruit, chewed, and swallowed. She held semi-eaten fruit above her head and declared it: "Sin."

Alhazred's Walls

Some obsessions well up and manifest in such a way as to be completely and utterly inescapable. I have found that the carnal sins, the desires of the body and of the flesh, are not only the most troublesome but also the most difficult to keep private. The flesh's peculiar nature requires the sensitive reflection of admiring eyes to caress each color soaked pore. Just as a peacock dances with feathers fanned, each feather full of a primeval need to attract and keep a mate's keen interest while evolution's grand design is perpetuated, urban youth bare ink in spring. In this lusty world of beast and bird, such markings prove to be doubly useful, having impact upon both the visually receptive mate and the skittish would be predators.

It is only natural to wish to become increasingly visually appealing. The desire to be admired and touched, to be stroked tenderly, approvingly, to work bare-chested on a hot spring day in the yard. Both will sexes taking notice. Minneapolis in spring sees both man and woman shed thick layers of wool, an impulse as primal as any beast's.

This annual ritual undertaken by the Twin Cities' urban residents exposes skin untouched the by sun's cosmic embrace and the bright colors set into flesh by talented tattoo artists.

Once such artist's designs were coveted above all others. He was said to have had a genius to rival the great masters of oil and canvas. With each masterpiece came a money back guarantee that ensured a collector's lifetime satisfaction. His shop's reputation had grown daily. Customers from all over the world had requested him. His waiting list, already years long, had continued to fill. Too busy painting skin, he had hired me to watch over the shop's daily needs, ensure health standards, hire lesser but superbly talented ink slingers, and handle whatever else arose out of the regular minutiae of his business.

My job description was vague, but I got to work in his shop, brush elbows with Hollywood and European royalty. I like to think that I was hired on for my attention to detail, skill as an accountant, and my ability to blend into his particular subculture. My compensation included a decent salary and housing above the shop across the hall from his apartment. I was attentive to his every whim at whatever hour. Artists are such truly fragile creatures. Many a night, he would call upon me in the hours just before dawn, hours too early for men who work late into the night, asking me to comfort his mind with my doting praise for his work.

He owned the entire building, a hideous aqua fishbowl of building just south of Downtown Minneapolis, at the intersection of three neighborhoods, Stevens Square, The Wedge, and Loring Park. After the economic revitalization of Uptown, the invasion of corporate chains, the influx of high-healed, short-skirt wearing man hunters, the locals had shifted away into these three communities. After purchasing the building, he kept the original name and allowed the sandwich and coffee joints that occupied the street level to remain.

While in his apartment, he would show me the wonders that haunted his sleep. These visions would force him from his bed to paint upon the walls of his studio. Picasso and Giger would have shuddered at such depictions of his dreamland. After each such occasion, which had seemed to be ever more frequent, I would, as instructed, document the designs with a digital camera, and then paint over them with the most delicate eggshell white.

These pictures were the basis for his tattoos and, by my hand, collected and archived. One collection was kept in the shop. The other was hidden away in local bank, securely stored in a safe deposit box of which I had held the only key. He had wanted it this way. I followed each of his instructions expertly, except for one. I kept a third collection of his works, a complete collection, for he would edit and delete certain images before he gave the camera over to me, on a flash drive that I wore around my neck. It was in the shape of an ankh, a symbol not out of place on my person, to the guests, or to my employer.

In my spare time, which if I had any complaints, is that I rarely had time to myself, I would organize his pictures and ponder them. It was my hope that these pictures would some day be my ticket to some modest notoriety. I had two conceptions for such a book. The first was obvious, but impractical to the volume of art, a complete works of

Alhazred. I had possessed more than six thousand photographs. The other was a selected volume of the pictures that he had wished deleted. These, ironic in my estimation, were his best imaginings.

The deleted photos contained marvels in which I could loose myself for hours. Rather than photographs of painting, they seemed more like the travel pictures that some tourist of a strange, alien landscape would take. They had an essence of exactness that eluded his other work and made those that he chose to keep seem lewd and cartoonish. It was if he had been to these places and wished to completely erase the experience. I couldn't understand why he would so exactingly eradicate these scenes from his portfolio. Surely, if he wanted to escape the life of a tattooist, which he sometimes spoke of doing, these painting would elevate him out from subculture obscurity and into the high snobbery of the world's art scene.

The most amazing aspect of these discarded paintings was that they were starting to take on what seemed like a panoramic view of a strange vista. In those spare moments that I could steal, I used new software to puzzle them together. It took some time before I found a pattern. However, when I did discover a logic to them, it had seemed as if I had found the border pieces of a children's jigsaw puzzle. There was a grotesque oily gray squiggle that ran thorough several of the paintings. Once I started focusing in on that detail, the pictures started to fall into place. I still have several hundred left, but I was closing in on what I felt would be a significant insight into his dreams. Perhaps enough would be revealed that I could help him find at least one unaided nights rest, and selfishly one for me.

Recently, I had stared to relish the sleepless nights when he would run into my room and shake me awake. I would lie fully clothed in wait. Some nights, even though I had help closed the shop around 2:00 AM, I found it increasingly difficult to sleep. I would pace in my apartment or listen at the door for him to rush over seeking my help. Each time, I would capture new pieces of the puzzle. I wondered if he knew what he was doing by deleting these pictures. My frustration with his waste grew each time I helped him white wash his walls. The loss of the originals weighed upon my consciousness like a gypsy curse, a curse of a fate unfulfilled, or worse... I must finish the puzzle. I must know what it is that he dreams of in paint, from what unholy source was he taped into that brought forth such a kaleidoscope of horrors.

My impatient agitation was becoming unbearable. There had appeared in the lower left hand corner the beginnings of what looked like a pair of Doc Martins poking out beneath blue jeans. The person, because what else would wear shoes, was standing upon a large rock in the middle of turbulent seas. I could make out the beginnings of a shoreline just beyond the rock. The perspective was all wrong. The buildings upon the distant shore stood out at peculiar angles and their bases seemed smaller than what should have been the attic, they almost resembled tentacles protruding out of the sand, but that seemed too queer even amongst the chaos of everything else. There was nothing that I could do but wait and hope he'd succumb to one his visions.

Then one night, after a few weeks of torturously peaceful ones, he roused me from my sleep, shaking me by the shoulders. He had never touched me before. He was shouting at the top of his lungs.

"Howie. Howie. Come on, wake up."

I must have been comatose. I was not normally that difficult to wake, being a very light sleeper. Sometimes the slightest bit of settling by the building would have me beside the bed, skittishly looking for what was the matter.

"Howie."

I finally came to enough to answer, "Wha...Al. Al, is that you?"

"Yes. Yes. Get up. I need you. Hurry." The look on his face was more sever than I was used to seeing. I'd seen him in a panic before, but nothing like this. His face was snarled and bestial, lips drawn tight. I clearly saw his fillings, in the lamp light. They sparkled like a nightmarish disco ball. His eyes said it all. They were wide and fully dilated, darting from me and to the shadows, searching, inspecting.

"I'll get the camera. It will only take..."

"No. No camera. No time. Just come."

He let go of my arm, and I felt the blood rush back into my hand. I felt the tingling, prickling sensation of a sleeping appendage waking. I waved it, trying to quicken its revival. Without throwing on cloths, I rushed through my apartment and into the hall after him. Whatever the matter was, it was urgent. In the back of my mind, the part that controls flight or fight, was trying to tell me something, but I had to see the paintings. I had to know if he had filled in any of the cursed gaps in the unfolding panorama.

Instead of waiting for me in his apartment, he was standing in the hall. He had with him a large bottle. I think it was Jack. He looked at me and shook his head. It seemed that some of the terror had gone out of him. I waited for him to give me leave to enter. Each moment was like an ice pick in my chest. What was he waiting for? Why was he just standing in the way? Let me enter damn it. Still, I waited.

I walked over to him and placed my hand on his shoulder. His eyes were open and searching, but it was as if no one was guiding his pupils, his person on autopilot. I took him by the shoulders and shook him.

"Howie."

"Yes." I waited.

"Howie. You are good friend to me."

"Yes. And you are good to me."

"Please, no pictures. Just wipe it all."

"Are you sure?" This must be what I was waiting for. It must be. I didn't want to rush him now. He was going to throw away an entire night's dream.

"Yes. And when you are done, take some time off. Go somewhere. I'm closing the shop for awhile. I need to..." He tailed off. He turned and staggered down the stairs without looking back clutching the bottle as if it contained some grand remedy for his current state.

I was so stunned at his words that I just stood there. I don't know how long I stood there, but it was long enough to begin to notice my nakedness. Now that he knew that I was going to take care of whatever it was in his apartment that had spooked him, I was free to retrieve cloths, painting supplies, and the camera. Retrieving these items took painful minutes, but I knew that if he returned to find me in his apartment without the painting supplies, he would be suspicious.

Taking cautious steps though his doorway, paint and brush in hand, I could feel an aura of ghastly dread, thick and heavy like wet wool, caress my skin. I could swear that the rings that lines the lobes of my ears vibrated and sung a high-pitched tune that I could not hope to name. That desperate tune should have been warning enough to wait upon dawn and the help of others, but I was his servant in all things. I was the only one he trusted to perform this task.

When I flipped on the lights, I must have accidentally dropped the paint bucket because it rolled tightly sealed into the next room after hitting the floor, but I paid it no mind. My attention was fixed upon the far wall, his usual dream canvas. The wall was covered in red ocher script that stretched far outside his typical frame to include all uncovered spaces upon each of the four walls in the living room.

I spun in circles trying to take it all in. The writing was like nothing that I had ever encountered. I moved to one section of the wall and traced the bizarre lines with my index finger. It had the looping and scrawling elements of Arabic, but it was not Arabic. Several of the shops lesser clients admired a certain actress' tattoo and sought reproductions cut into their skin in the vain hope that they too would become an object of male desire. Lettering had become a craze as of late, more and more walk-ins wanted letters instead of pictures. He would never lower himself to ink such flash. It was beneath his talent.

Remembering where I was and what I should be about, I quickly started to document each wall. As I came to the door to the next room, I noticed that one of the words curved around the door jam. I passed through and flipped on the light. His bedroom walls were in the same state as the living room, except as I looked up at the ceiling the writing was replaced with a large elaborate depiction of what must have been a gothic-styled gate.

The gate looked as if it were to have swung out, or do to its location on the ceiling, up. The painting had delicate looking hinges along the outsides located at the top, bottom, and at the midpoints. Each door was covered in gruesome faces that looked as if they were trying to stretch through the bars. In the center, holding the gate shut was a large lock engraved with what looked like a childishly simple drawing of a leafless branch.

Then I saw it. It was there. I had almost missed it among everything else. There at the bottom of the gate was that same gray line that had enabled me to begin organizing the other photos. I could now see in my mind where this piece would fit. I took the picture and quickly transferred it to my flash drive. I wanted to sprint back across to my apartment and put this picture into place, to see if it unlocked any new revelations, but I couldn't. I had work to do here. I had to document the rest of the house before he came to check on my progress.

I quickly moved from room to room. I found a few other pictures just as gruesome located on the ceilings in the kitchen, bathroom, and living room. It was amazing that he had been able to cover every surface in his apartment in such a short time and in such exacting detail. It couldn't have been more than two or three hours after we had closed the shop, when he had roused me from bed. The more I thought about it the more impossible it seemed.

Taking the last photo in the bathroom, I snuck back across the hall and downloaded the pictures onto my hard drive. Then I backed them up on the flash dive around my neck. I wiped the camera's memory and placed it back on my bookcase. I was overcome with a sense of curiosity that forced me to begin cropping and editing those pictures, trying to add them to the terrifying puzzle.

Several of the odd pictures fit into the puzzle, completing a good majority, except for the legs atop the rock. My attention focused on the gate from his bedroom. After adding the other pieces, it was no longer obvious where the gate would fit. I tried resizing it and floating it over the rest of the puzzle, but it did not seem to want to comply. Frustrated, I set that photo aside and started to inspect the strange writing that dominated his walls.

I still could not make anything of those letters. The language and meaning fully escaped me. At least with the help of the latest graphic software, I was able to quickly order the pictures into some semblance of logical progression, which meant that there was a recognizable grammar within those loops and swirls. Decryption would have to wait, it was getting late and I had a long job ahead of me.

While white washing his walls and ceilings, a thought had occurred to me while working on a small segment where the living room wall met the door jam to his bedroom. The thought was less idea and more word, a word that I knew I had never heard spoken aloud or seen written, but it seemed so logical. It was what I would eventually call the selection of paintings that I had been collecting. It was such a simple word, but held all the meaning and terror that I could ever hope for in a title.

"I will call it, Necronomicon."

I must have said it aloud because as my mouth closed, I bit my tongue hard enough to cause it to bleed. I knew that he kept tissues on his nightstand next to his bed. As I stood there in the lamplight holding my bloody tongue, I heard a rusty creaking from somewhere nearby, somewhere overhead.

Still holding my tongue, I looked up, and to my astonishment, the gate had swung open reveling a picture of a turbulent sea crashing upon a large rock. There, standing there on the rock was my perfect likeness. Out stretched in my arms, I held a giant ghastly tome as if I was reading from it. Seeing myself there, past the open gate, standing upon the rock, took from me any last scrap of sanity I possessed.

I ran from the room and smashed my computer on the floor in my room. I then tossed the desktop out my bedroom window causing the building's alarms to sound. Looking out of the destroyed window, the pavement seemed to move, and I lost my balance and tumbled headfirst out into the open air.

Do to some stroke of luck, I landed on my legs, breaking both into hundreds of pieces the doctors tell me. The doctors also tell me that I will, with much physical therapy, be able to walk again with the aid of a cane. In my many nights of morphine-induced rest, I have had time to think upon the events of that night. I must have seen my image in error. It was impossible that I would have found my way into his dreams, doubly so, that a painting, fixed with the permanence of ink in skin, could alter so drastically.

Yes, officer, as I said, there were two copies of all his photos, all his paintings. Well, yes, excluding those puzzle piece-like horrors I saved from deletion. Wait, I don't remember destroying my flash drive. It must still be some where inside the shop. No, I don't remember taking it off. I never took it off, except to bathe or shower. All those viable and grotesque shapes, those too real imaginings are still out in the world. Dear God, when I fell... I swear it was around my neck, but since I was not in a right frame of mind... Yes, its whereabouts are perfectly questionable.

The Methuselah Project

The value of old age depends upon the person who reaches It. To some men of early performance it is useless. To others, who are late to develop, it just enables them to finish the job. —Thomas Hardy

Prologue

Pentagon, 2160

"Now that we have it, what should we do with it?"

"File it along with everything else."

"You sure? Any special classification?"

"No."

"Sir?"

"If we label it TOP SECRET, it will have to be read again at some point to determine if it can de declassified."

"I follow. Hide it in the open.

The Interviews

10/25/2150 – Tessa Roy

TR: I didn't choose this.

M1: None of us did. Tell me when you realized your gift.

TR: Gift? We're been rounded up and numbered. How could you?

M1: It will be easier for both of us if you answer without the hostility. Please. Tell me when you realized your gift.

TR: I hate you. I really do.

M1: I know. Please.

TR: It was my fortieth birthday party. My father and a few friends knew that I loved old cars. The tail fins. The stripes. The leather bench seats made for sex. My father picked me up at 3:30. It was going to be just him and me. I had just divorced my second husband. The paperwork had gone though two days earlier. My father surprised me by pulling up in a classic black 1956 Cadillac El Dorado Seville with chrome rails and a pearl hardtop. We drove up the PCH along the coast until we got to a lookout, and he parked the car and got out.

M1: So he told you?

TR: He had pictures from my twenty-fifth birthday. Close ups.

M1: That's not unusual. Most parents took pictures so that they could sue if the results were not what they desired.

TR: As you can see, it worked.

M1: How old are you?

TR: Fuck you!

M1: I have questions that I have to ask everyone. How old are you?

TR: They already know. So, fuck you.

M1: Says here you were born in 2054.

TR: Yeah, that's right.

M1: Have you used aliases?

TR: Of course.

M1: Can you list them for me?

TR: I have to, right?

M1: Good behavior helps.

TR: Susan Bradshaw, Kelsey Thompson, Anaya Hout. Anaya Hout was my favorite. She knew how to live.

M1: Did you have investments?

TR: Yes. I think that when you realize what is ahead of you, at some point you decide working is for the birds.

M1: That's the truth.

TR: How'd they catch you? You were supposed to be a myth.

M1: Answer the rest of my questions and I'll tell you.

TR: Deal.

M1: Did you have any children?

TR: Two. Why?

M1: How are they?

TR: Dead.

M1: It is a known side effect.

The Roundups

Miami, 2148

Sarah knew that they would come. She had thought it through several years before, when she had found out that she was one of them. Sarah kept her head down and did not look at the others. She tried not to rattle her own chains. She just did not think that it would have been today. Not that today was less likely than any other day; it was just that she had expected a sign or portent like darkening skies, strong winds, salt brine in the air, signals that a hurricane is near. At the very least, a breaking news brief, something that would have said, *run, Sarah, run.*

Sarah had a plan. She kept the trunk of her Lincoln fully stocked: tent, clothes, food and water enough for a week, fake IDs, and ten thousand in cash. When she spotted the first dark cloud on the horizon, she would set fire to her beach house and drive into the sunset, as she made her way into the memories of those she had known, to start again somewhere in the Midwest. She had thought that this time she would try being the wife of a Baptist minister, living on the straight and narrow. She loved gospel music so it wouldn't be that big of a stretch. She had learned that she had to reinvent herself every ten to twenty years anyway.

The reality was that there had been no warning. She had just finished making breakfast, eggs over easy on wheat toast with real maple syrup. She settled down on the porch, watching the surf break against the sand and the spring-break-bodies strip down to muscle and lotion. Which one today? Perhaps the blond with blue trunks. He couldn't be more than twenty-two. Sarah watched as his buddies pulled up their surfboards and made their way into the water, lean and stiff. If there was one thing that life had taught her, it was that you took what you wanted when you wanted it. It might not be there at second glance.

She put her food down half-eaten. She stripped down to a string bikini with red and white hearts. She let her auburn hair fall down her tan shoulders and back. Leaving her flip-flops on her deck, Sarah could feel eyes follow her as she made her way down to where the water kissed the beach. Men were so easy. She pointed at her prey, "You there."

Straddling his board, he pointed at his chest.

Sarah nodded and waved him in. She could see him look to his friends for support. The longhaired skinny one splashed him. He started to paddle in. She watched the muscles in his arms and back work.

He came out of the water. "Hey."

"I think you're what I want for breakfast." She held out her hand to him as she had to so many others.

He took a step back and looked over his shoulders. His friends whistled and shouted. "Do I know you?" he asked.

She took his hand and started back up the beach. She looked over her shoulder at him. She'd picked well. "Do you want to?"

"Sure. I'm Robert."

"Nice to meet you Robert," she kissed the tips of his fingers.

He squirmed a little. "And you are?"

"Does it matter?" She bit his pinky finger.

"No, I guess not."

She smiled. She'd chosen well.

"It's just a little…" He planted his board at in front of her porch, "this never happens to me."

"Oh sure," she ran her nails down his chest, "you can't fool me." She led him by the hand up to her house. Sarah opened the door and stepped through. She felt a sharp strike at the base of her neck before slumping forward onto the floor.

The Decisions

Project Future, Southern Texas, 2156

You stand in a row in a crowd of people that you have never met, but with whom you share a singular fate. As you look around, no one looks a day older than thirty. They seem to have accepted their lot as if this were inevitable from the beginning, a long game of choices and chances. Some hang their heads and slump their shoulders. Others stand straight, heads held high as if they were royalty being led to the guillotine. There are more than you thought there would have been. Someone said there were fifteen hundred or more.

The one you know as M1 takes the stage. He was kind enough when interviewing you. He knew all the right questions. He had on a dark purple uniform with strange symbols and markings. The only thing familiar about it was the strand of five gold stars on each lapel.

"You all stand accused of a crime you had no choice in committing."

You listen to him as he goes on about how his father had wanted to live forever, witness history and *be* history. He claims to be have been born in the late twentieth century, which doesn't seem possible.

"Each and every one of you is at least fifty years or older, but you look no older than twenty-five. In fifty, even two-hundred years from now, you will still look no older than you do today. Even though your parents were well-meaning and had the best of intentions for you when they signed up for the Methuselah Project, they did not, could not, see the true scope of what would happen to you. Some of you know this by experience, never being able to grow old with a loved one, not being able to have children, having to move and reinvent yourself every 20 to 30 years."

You're still too young to know these pains, just turning fifty a few days ago. You never felt it necessary to settle down anywhere or with any one woman. It didn't feel natural to stay in one place. You never thought about your health and your looks in that way before.

"Some of us have learned to use the system to our advantage. Invest safe, invest a lot. Wait. We have the time. But now, we have been rounded up to be executed by a religious government that believes we are living-blasphemies against their god. They blame us for the weather, failed crops, the Great Flood of 2110."

You'd seen something on TV once about the growing animosity of the religious and their belief that genetic engineering was the greatest sin man had ever conceived. Something about Genesis 6:30 and God's decree that man shouldn't live longer than 120 years. If this guy is who he says he is, he'd be more than 150 years old, but he doesn't look any older than you.

"However, we cannot die. You may not know this. I have been forced to work with the government. Tests were run, trying to find a way kill me and our kind, to exterminate our race. They went as far as to incinerate my body. Nothing works. Eventually, I was again, alive."

You don't believe it.

"Once the government determined without a doubt our impervious nature, they gave me a choice. To that end, I have helped the government track you all down and bring you here to Project Future. If we are truly immortal, as my father had hoped, we have a responsibility to the future and to the past. I'm asking for your help..."

You don't believe it

The Beginnings

Ceresco, Nebraska, 1982

"It works?"

Harold Johns nodded his head. "Subjects nine through the end of the series are now two years old and showing no signs of aging." Harold was nervous. He didn't have the words to make things sound good. It was always just the facts. He knew he had to make his research sound exciting or it could mean his job.

"Two years?"

Harold pushed up his glasses, "The fruit fly lives an average life of 20 to 30 days depending on environmental conditions. Here," Harold flourished his arm indicating the jars, "I have more than a hundred examples proving that my research works." He let his arm fall to the side.

"It says in your report that that there are side effects."

Harold smiled. The side effects were going to make him rich even if no one wanted the intended effect. He watched the man in uniform carefully. He could see that he was interested. His eyes were fully dilated. "Here, let me show you." Harold took jar number thirty-four off the shelf. He opened the lid. Using a swab coated with honey he trapped the fly on the tip. "Now watch closely."

"What am I looking for?"

Harold killed the fly using his thumb and index finger.

"Hey. Those are valuable."

Harold dropped the fly back into the jar and handed it over. "Just watch. Here." He handed the uniform a magnified glass. "Watch closely."

"I see a fly."

Harold pushed a needle into the tube piercing the fly through its back. He then jabbed it a few more times just to make sure.

"You killed it."

"Keep watching, please."

The fly lay there for a few seconds more before its wings started to twitch. Then it was up and flying about again.

"How is that possible?" The uniform's jaw hung slack.

Harold took the jar and placed it back on the shelf among the others. "It has to do with the body's electro..."

"Keep it simple!"

"The spark of life."

"Spark?"

Harold slipped a small wire into jar twenty-nine. "Watch." The tiny fly touched the wire for just a second and a small bulb lit up at the other end. "Their genetic makeup has been enhanced with nanites."

"You mean they have living machines in them."

"Well," Harold winced, "Yes and no." He folded his hands across his chest. "I like to think of them as..."

"Yes or no, living machines."

Harold made a choice. "No."

"Good. Can't have machines replace humans, now can we?"

"Would you like some coffee?"

"No time."

Harold watched him walk toward the door. It was time to be bold. "Can I expect further funding?"

"You'll be seeing me again, Dr. Johns."

The Methuselahs

Lincoln, Nebraska, 1991

"Isn't he cute?" Maggie Johns said, trying to keep her eyes open and to catch her breath. She was wrapped in white, her red hair damp with sweat.

The nurse asked, "What's his name?" pen in hand.

Maggie looked up at her husband. "Harold?" She knew already what he would say. His obsession with longevity and living forever demanded it. It still surprised her to hear him say it out loud.

"Harold Methuselah Johns."

"Very nice," said the nurse. "I'll give you two a couple of minutes, but then we need little Harold to run some tests."

Maggie smiled and touched his little nose. "So, we'll call him Junior."

"I was thinking M1."

"You shit." Maggie tried to sit up. She was so tired. "Tell me you didn't!"

"He'll live forever Maggie. I gave him a gift that can never be taken away. It is all that I have to offer."

"You didn't. You fucking didn't." Maggie began to sob. "When? When did you curse our child?"

"It's not a curse."

"When damn it!"

"That night you came crying back to me. Said, you wanted a family."

"Two years ago?" She looked at Junior. "We weren't pregnant then?"

"The serum needs to be infused with ovum before encountering sperm for the effects to take hold."

She watched him take a step forward. He removed a syringe from his lab coat. He pricked her arm.

"This will purge the Methuselah serum from your system."

Maggie watched as he put the empty syringe in to the medial and biohazard waste bin. "Fuck you Harold. I'll expose you!"

"Maggie, please. He will be the future. He will fix everything that with our short lives we could never see through."

Maggie screamed. The monitors went wild and people rushed into the room.

"What's happening? Help her!"

Maggie felt Junior being lifted out of her hands. As her body shook, she saw Junior running though an alley. His pursuers wore fatigues and carried rifles. He had an unkempt-bushy red beard and wore tattered clothing. As she slipped into unconsciousness, she vowed to herself to take Junior away from Harold, far away.

About the Author

Aaron M. Wilson lives in Beloit, WI with his wife and daughter. He is also the author of *The Many Lives of Inez Wick*, as well as other short stories and poems scattered here and there.

For updates:

- Homepage - www.soullessmachine.com
- Twitter - twitter.com/SoullessMachine

About the Cover Artist

Kristen Nelson is a graphic and web designer living in Minneapolis, Minnesota. She received her Bachelor of Arts in Advertising from the University of St. Thomas. She is currently taking classes at the University of Phoenix towards a Bachelor of Science in Information Technology.

Her cat, Pantalaimon, tends to keep her company through any design she creates and often helps out by laying in front of the computer as she works. In her spare time, she enjoys playing games, cooking, and, of course, creating fun designs.

To see more of Kristen Nelson's work:

* Homepage - www.thekristinnelson.com

www.ingramcontent.com/pod-product-compliance
Lightning Source LLC
Chambersburg PA
CBHW020431180626
46812CB00003B/1180